EVERYTHING
BEGINS & ENDS
AT THE KENTUCKY CLUB

EVERYTHING
BEGINS & ENDS
AT THE KENTUCKY CLUB

Stories by Benjamin Alire Sáenz

CINCO PUNTOS PRESS
www.cincopuntos.com

He Went To Be With the Women first appeared in *Narrative.com*. *Sometimes the Rain* first appeared in *11/11*.

FIRST EDITION 10 9 8 7 6 5 4 3 2 1

Library of Congress Cataloging-in-Publication Data

Sáenz, Benjamin Alire.
  Everything begins & ends at the Kentucky Club / by Benjamin Alire Sáenz.
-- 1st ed.
  p. cm.
ISBN 978-1-935955-32-0 (alk. paper), E-book ISBN 978-1-935955-33-7
  I. Title.
PS3569.A27E94 2012
813'.54--dc23

2012004532

COVER PHOTO AND BOOK DESIGN BY ANTONIO CASTRO H.
Thanks to Lostandtaken.com for the back cover, flap, and spine texture.

Ohh, this cover took a lot of doing. First it was going to be Fred and Patty Dalbin on the cover with Rich Wright in a spectacular old photo supplied by Vanessa Johnson. Much discussion ensued on that one. How we would have loved to see our friends hit the big-time. But it was not to be. Bruce Berman took some great shots and one made an almost perfect cover. But ultimately it was this image made by Antonio Castro that evoked the essence of Ben's stories. Antonio went to the Kentucky Club in Juarez with Ben and Bobby on one of those dreamy afternoon visits you can only have when you cross over to the other side.

I want to listen to my heart as it beats like a
piece of music in a silence that waits to be broken.

TABLE OF CONTENTS

HE HAS GONE TO BE WITH THE WOMEN

I.

The slant of morning light made him look like he was about to catch on fire.

Every Sunday he was there, a singular, solitary figure—but not sad and not lonely. And not tragic. He became the main character of a story I was writing in my head. *Some people are so beautiful that they belong everywhere they go.* That was the first sentence of the story.

I always noticed what he was reading: Dostoyevsky, Kazantzakis, Faulkner. He was in love with serious literature. And tragedy. Well, he lived on the border. And on the border you could be in love with tragedy without being tragic.

He drank his coffee black. Not that I knew that with any certainty.

Sometimes, I could see that he'd just come in from a run, his dark wavy hair wild, half-wet with sweat.

He was thin and had to shave twice a day. But he only shaved once. There was always that shadow on his face. Even in the morning light he appeared to be half-hidden.

I don't know how long I'd been noticing him. A year. Longer.

He was a creature of habit. Not so different from a monk. Not so different from me.

Our eyes never met though I had memorized the color of his eyes.

I never lingered at the coffee shop—but there was always a line on Sunday mornings. I was grateful for the wait. It gave me the opportunity to glance at him as he read his book. I wanted to walk up to him and ask him what he thought of Kazantzakis. I imagined me blurting out that no one read him anymore. I imagined him smiling at me.

I never ordered coffee.

I would drop in to pick up the Sunday *New York Times* and drive back home to drink my own free-trade, fresh-ground coffee. I always ran into someone I knew. People were so nice to me. Always. *Hello Mr. De la Tierra you're looking good Mr. De la Tierra what are you working on now Mr. De la Tierra so nice to see you Mr. De la Tierra.* The fact that so many people knew who I was had never given me much comfort. If anything, it made me feel more alone. And anyway, nobody knew who I was. Not even me.

2.

Sundays were mine. The rest of the week belonged to my responsibilities, my writing, my family, my friends, my commitments. I could give all my days up for everything else. But not Sundays. I loved the quiet softness of that day. I'd read the paper and inhale the stillness of the neighborhood that was resting from the punishing week. It was that kind of neighborhood.

And then one Sunday we spoke.

I was standing at the counter of the coffee shop, *New York Times* in hand, deciding. Croissant? Maybe a scone? I was hungry.

"You never buy a cup of coffee."

Even before I turned around, I knew it was him.

"No," I said.

"You don't like coffee?"

"My coffee is waiting for me at home."

"So your coffee is like a wife?"

"Yes," I said, "exactly like a wife."

"And do you?"

"Do I?"

"Have a wife?"

I stuck out my left hand. No ring.

He didn't smile but I thought he wanted to. I paid for my paper.

He ordered a tall coffee of the day. I was right about him drinking his coffee black. His voice was deep and friendly. It was nice—his accent. I wanted to keep talking. But there was never anything to say when it mattered so much to say something. "You like newspapers," he said.

"Yes."

"They're the past. And they're all lies."

I held up my newspaper. "It's not *El Diario*."

"Are you one of those?"

I looked into his smiling face. "One of those?"

He laughed. "One of those Mexicans who hates other Mexicans?"

"No. I don't suffer from that disease."

"What do you suffer from?"

I didn't say anything. I looked into his chocolate eyes. I think I was looking for *suffering*.

"You're not really Mexican," he said.

"Not Mexican. Not American. Fucked. That's the disease I suffer from."

We found ourselves sitting outside. The morning was cool. The wind was back, the wind that was in love with El Paso, the wind that refused to leave us to enjoy the sun.

"You're cold," he said.

"I forgot my jacket."

"We can go inside."

"No," I said. We studied each other. My eyes weren't as dark as his. Pedestrian brown. "I don't live far from here."

He was thinking.

"I'm not looking for a hook-up." Just as the words came out of my mouth, I realized they sounded like an accusation. I was sorry for having said anything.

"No," he said, "not a man like you." He smiled. "My name is Javier."

"Javier," I said, "I'm—"

"Everybody knows who you are."

"Nobody knows who I am."

He laughed, Javier who drank his coffee black. "Tell me. I want to hear you say your name."

"Juan Carlos."

"Juan Carlos," he repeated. "Where do you live?"

"Sunset Heights."

He tapped his paper cup. "Interesting neighborhood."

3.

"It's a beautiful place," he said. He was studying one of my paintings.

"It was built in 1900."

"Ten years before the Revolution."

"More than a hundred years ago."

"And here we are. One real Mexican and one Mexican who's American."

"My grandfather was born here," I said.

"My grandfather was born in Israel," he said.

"So I'm more Mexican than you are."

"I wouldn't say so."

That made me laugh.

He was still studying the painting. "Why is the man grieving?"

"He's tired of war."

"I'm tired of war too."

"Israel," I said. "Israel and Mexico. A true child of war."

"Yes. Maybe that's what circumcision is all about."

That made me laugh.

"You too," he said. "I think you're circumcised."

"Such a tragedy," I said, "to lose your foreskin. Not that I'm Jewish. You don't mind, do you—that I'm not Jewish?"

"I didn't say I was Jewish."

"But you said your father was born in Israel."

"He was an Iraqi born in Israel. He fled to Mexico. He married my grandmother in Chihuahua. He was killed in a bar. He liked to fight."

"A child of war," I repeated.

He laughed. "So why are you circumcised?"

"I have no idea. I woke up one day and there it all was."

"Real Mexican men aren't circumcised."

"It's settled then. I'm not a real Mexican."

He knew the conversation was making me uncomfortable.

"You don't enjoy talking about circumcision?"

"It's never come up in a conversation before."

"And do you like to fight?"

"No. I don't like to fight."

"Certainly you're not a Mexican," he said.

I took the paper cup out of his hand and replaced it with a fresh cup of coffee. I let him drink out of my favorite mug, the one with Van Gogh's face on it.

"You didn't lie."

"About what?"

"Your coffee was waiting for you."

"I always put on the coffee before I go get my newspaper."

"What do you like about newspapers?"

"The world's a big place."

"And you need a newspaper to tell you that?"

"Yes, I think so."

"Really?"

"It gives me the specifics."

"The world you live in can give you all the specifics you need."

"No."

"Yes."

Already we were arguing.

"I need facts."

"What for?"

"To help me form an opinion."

"You don't know what you think?"

"I'm not always right."

He laughed. "You study me," he said.

"Study you?"

"When you walk into the coffee house, you study me."

"You seem oblivious."

"I don't know that word."

"You seem not to notice anything except the book you're reading."

"Carlos, I notice." He had a pensive look on his face.

"That means you study me too."

"Yes."

"Why would you do that?"

"Why wouldn't I?"

"Javier, you're beautiful. And me? Not so beautiful. And your English is perfect."

"Perfect but with an accent."

"Which makes it even more perfect."

"You're something better than beautiful," he said.

"What's better than beautiful?"

"Interesting. Interesting is much better than beautiful." He reached over and ran his fingers across my cheek. His hands were rough. His fingers were calloused.

Maybe he played the guitar.

I wanted to kiss his fingers.

"You're quiet," he said.

"If I don't say anything, I'll stay interesting."

He ran his fingers through my salt and pepper hair.

"I'm older than you are," I said.

He kissed me.

I kissed him back.

4.

We sat on the balcony and drank our coffee—and listened to the rain.

"I don't know you," I said.

"What do you want to know?"

So he told me. About how he was caring for his uncle who was dying of lung cancer, about how he had helped care for his aunt who was paralyzed in an accident. About how he came every weekend from Juárez—Friday night till Sunday night—and other times whenever he could. About how he worked as a chauffeur for the U.S. Consulate in Juárez, and how he'd lived with his uncle and aunt who lived on Florence Street so that he would be able to go to school, and how they'd passed for his parents, and how he went home on weekends for twelve years of his life to stay with his mom who worked as a social worker, his mother who had a passion for working with transvestites, about how his father had been killed and had maybe left another family in Chicago or Los Angeles or Chihuahua (I wasn't the only one who made up things about other people). About how his aunt had died of cancer and how he'd helped his uncle take care of things, and how he took care of him now. But only on weekends.

"Do you love him?"

"He was good to me. My aunt was hard, but not him. He was soft. Can you say that in English? Soft?"

"Yes." I leaned over and kissed him. God, he was beautiful. That wasn't just a story I was making up.

"I didn't like my aunt," he said. He pulled out a cigarette. "Do you mind?"

"No. I don't mind."

"Would you like one?"

"I quit years ago."

"Why?'

"I can't remember."

"Are you a man who has amnesia about certain things?"

"*Cuando me conviene.*"

He laughed.

I watched him light his cigarette. I remembered how once, in a bar, a woman had walked up to me as I smoked a cigarette and told me I was beautiful. She kissed me. I let her tongue linger in my mouth. She tasted of cognac and cherry.

He let out the smoke through his nose. "Are you sure you don't want to start smoking again?"

"No. I want to start something new, something I've never done before." I watched him smoke. "So you didn't like your aunt."

"I didn't like her—but I loved her. She was so hard on people."

"Some people are like that," I said.

"You're not," he said.

"How do you know?"

"I've read your books."

"They're just books. You don't know anything about me."

He put out his cigarette. He ran his fingers through my salt and pepper hair. He kissed me. "I make up stories about you," he said.

I wish now I would have told him that I made up stories about him too.

5.

"¿Tienes hambre? I can cook something."

"Somehow I knew you liked to cook."

"Something you made up about me?"

"No, there's a lot of cooking in your novels."

"Well, people have to eat. Even people in novels."

He laughed. "I like the people in your novels."

"They're mostly fucked up."

"That's what I like about them." He looked at his watch.

"That's a beautiful watch."

"It was my father's."

"You need to go?"

He nodded. "I need to get back to my uncle. We always eat Sunday dinner together."

"Do you take him out?"

"Those days are gone. He used to love to go out. He would laugh and tell me about how life used to be for him. Now, he won't go out. He's afraid. Before, the only thing he was afraid of was my aunt. Now, he's like a boy. He cries. He reads the newspapers. He thinks he's living in Juárez. I tell him that we're in El Paso, that he's safe. But he doesn't believe me. He's afraid to go out. *Nos matan*, he says. I try to tell him that no one's going to hurt us—but it's no use. Every time I go out he tells me to be careful."

"And are you careful?"

"I'm not afraid of getting killed. Are you?"

"I don't live in Juárez."

"There are murders in every city."

I didn't want to get into an argument. Not about this. What good was that? And he knew Juárez better than I did. "You're right," I said.

"I just learned something else about you."

"What?"

"You're not a very good liar."

"I used to be." I wondered what look I was wearing on my face. "I would be afraid, I think, if I were you."

"What good is being afraid, Carlos?"

"No good at all," I said.

He studied my face.

I wanted to kiss him again. Maybe he would kiss me. Maybe I would just stand there feeling like a perfect idiot. I wasn't any good at any of this. I never had been. Some men were graceful when they loved. I was tentative and awkward.

"What?" He looked at me.

"Nothing."

"You were studying me again."

"Yes."

"I don't mind. I like the way you look at me."

"I could look at you for a long time," I said.

"You can kiss me again," he said.

He bowed his head and looked down. He was shy. Or maybe he was just humble. That's the one thing I hadn't made up about him—that he was humble. That he was sweet. That he was decent. Good-looking men were rarely any of those things.

I kissed him again.

He whispered my name. I wondered how my name felt on his tongue.

"Javier," I whispered back. "Do you know how long it's been since I've kissed anyone?"

He looked up at me. "Does it matter?"

"Kissing is serious business."

He kissed me again. "That didn't seem so serious, did it?"

"Yes," I said. "It did."

We didn't speak for a long time.

"I have to go," he whispered. "He's waiting for me."

"You'll cook for him?"

"Yes."

"I confess to being jealous of your uncle."

"You're not a jealous man," he said.

"Maybe I am."

"No."

He was so certain of who I was. I didn't want him to leave. He stepped closer. I started to say something but he placed his finger on my lips. I didn't really know what I was going to say. And anyway, sometimes it didn't matter, the things we said. It just didn't matter.

He didn't want a ride home. "My uncle doesn't live far—I want to walk." Maybe he needed some time to think. *About me*. Maybe. I wanted to stop. I wanted to stop writing the story of who he was and what he was thinking. Writing that story was starting to hurt.

When he left, I listened to his footsteps as he made his way down the stairs. I rushed out onto the balcony and watched him walk down the street. He turned around when he reached the corner. He waved. "I knew you'd be standing there," he yelled.

I didn't yell anything back.

I just stood there, leaning on the railing to the balcony. And watched him as he disappeared into the horizon of the city.

6.

Monday morning, I got this text from him: *I thought about you when I woke up this morning.* I read the text and then re-read it. And then re-read it again.

I felt like a school boy reading a note from a girl. No. A note from a boy.

I didn't know how to answer his text. I only engaged in the practice because my nephews and nieces demanded it of me. We wrote silly and affectionate things to each other. But this was different. Finally around noon, I texted him back. *Stay safe.* That's what I wrote. That's when it occurred to me that I was afraid. I didn't like to think of Javier walking the streets of Juárez, doing an errand, going to a store and getting killed, randomly for no reason. What good does it do to be afraid? He was right. Of course, he was right. But so many people had left already. Why couldn't he leave too? I knew the answer to that question even before I asked it. He wasn't the leaving kind. He loved his Juárez. I could see that in his eyes, in his unshaven face, in the way he moved and talked. I could almost taste his love for that poor and wretched city in his kisses. It enraged me that Juárez had become so chaotic and violent and capricious, a city hungry for the blood of its own people. How had this happened? I was sick to death of it, sick to death of the body count, sick to death that every killing went unprosecuted and unpunished. You could kill anybody. And what would happen? Nothing. The fucking city no longer cared who was killed. Soon, they would just be stepping over the bodies. *Stay safe. Stay safe. Stay safe.*

7.

The next Sunday, he appeared at my door. It was early. "They admitted my uncle into the hospital last night."

"You look tired," I said. And he did look tired. Tired and sad, his white shirt wrinkled.

"I slept in a chair in his room."

We walked up the stairs into my apartment.

"I like your world," he said as he stared at the new painting I was working on. He stared at the words on my computer. "Were you writing?"

"Yes."

"You write on Sundays?"

"It's like going to Mass."

He smiled. "So this is communion."

"Something like that."

"What are you writing?"

"A poem."

"About what?"

"About what's going on in Juárez."

"Why would you want to write about that?"

"Juárez is an obsession."

"Why?"

"Because it's a part of me."

"You don't live there."

"We're all one city, Javier."

"That's shit, Carlos." I liked the anger in his voice. "You think the fucking border doesn't matter?"

There are a lot of things I could have said, wanted to say, but the border was there and we lived on different sides of it. What good were utopian ideologies about borderless worlds from a writer of political poems? What good was an argument with a beautiful man?

He smiled. "It's not you I'm mad at."

"I know."

"Don't write about Juárez. Write about something beautiful."

"That's not what I do, Javier."

"I know. Your books are getting sadder."

"There's a lot to be sad about."

"That's strange. Because you're not a sad man."

"No, I don't think I am."

"Why aren't you sad?"

"I used to be. I'm better now."

"And so you're happy?"

"Right now I'm happy."

"You're complicated."

"I've gone from being interesting to being complicated?"

He laughed. He put his head on my shoulder. He started to cry.

"He's going to die," he whispered. "I don't have anyone." His tears were soaking my shirt. I wanted to taste them, bathe in them, drown in them. "He's going to die." He kept repeating it over and over.

I never knew what to say when people cried. Especially men. Before my father died, I used to sit and listen to him weep. Sometimes I'd hold his hand. I was in love with that picture in my head: me holding my father's hand. So that's what I did. I took Javier's hand and held it. I led him to my bedroom. "You should sleep," I said. "You're tired."

He lay down on the bed. I took off his shoes.

He stared at the small mural I'd started on one of the walls. "I like it."

"I just started it."

"Leave it like that."

"It's only a sky."

"It's beautiful. Just a sky. Leave it like that." He was tired and he was whispering.

"Sleep," I said.

It was cold outside. The wind was picking up and the clouds were gathering like a flock of unwelcome crows. I hated crows. They were mean and selfish and liked to dance around and gloat when they caught a lizard. I stepped out into the balcony and took a breath. I thought of smoking a cigarette—but I didn't want to go back to that time. I wasn't so young anymore. I'd made so many mistakes. Smoking was the least of it. I wouldn't go back.

I walked back inside and decided to make a potato soup. I cleaned some potatoes, cubed them, cubed some onions, threw them into a pot and added some salt, some pepper, some garlic, chopped up some cilantro. A poor man's soup. Not that I was poor, but making the soup reminded me of my mother. I loved her. And loved her soup.

I walked into the bedroom and watched Javier sleep. He was having a bad dream. He was shaking and muttering, but I couldn't make out what he was saying. I sat on the bed and placed my hand on his chest. "It's only a dream," I whispered. He woke up, startled. There was that look of fear in his eyes. And then that look, that look of letting go.

"It's okay," I said.

I climbed into bed with him. He leaned into me. It was getting dark. I loved and hated winter. I felt his breath on my neck, felt the words he whispered, "Tell me something about you I don't know."

So I told him. About how my two older brothers had died in a car accident and how they'd left behind seven children between them. Seven children and two grieving, broken-hearted women who'd adored them. About how my father had suffered for years from depression and high blood pressure and Parkinson's and diabetes and how he had suffered a stroke that left him brain dead and how I'd taken him off the machine that kept him breathing. About the woman I'd loved and hurt and left. About the man who'd loved me, about how I'd never had the courage to return his love. About a young woman I'd met in London who had eyes as blue as a summer sky and how I'd lost myself in them when I imagined myself to be a man but was nothing more than a stupid adolescent. About how I picked onions long before I was old enough to have a legal job and dreamed of becoming something more than a worker with a bent back. About the scar I had across my chest because a barbed wire fence had ripped my skin as if it were no more than a piece of paper when I was a careless boy.

I didn't even notice my own tears.

I felt his hand on my face. "Tears taste like the ocean. Did you know that?"

"Sometimes I think the ocean is made of tears."

He put his finger on my lips. "Your life is better than your novels."

I took his hand and stared into his palm. I sat up on the bed. "My novels are filled with beautiful men. The kind of men that I will never be."

"You're not sad. You're just hurt."

"We're all hurt."

And then, there we were, undressing each other. He ran his finger on my scar and kissed it. I stared at his perfect body. But I was most in love with his face, with his eyes, with that look of want that transcended the cheap desires of the body. I led him to the shower. I washed his back, his hair, his feet, his legs. "Let me," he said. That was hard for me—to let him wash me. To let him touch me. But I let him.

8.

We listened to Miles Davis, ate potato soup and drank wine. I wondered if it could be like this for us. For me and him. For Javier and Juan Carlos.

I watched him eat. I wondered if a man like me could ever fill the kind of hunger that lived inside of him.

"The soup is good," he said.

"It's nothing complicated."

"It takes a lifetime to get good at something this simple."

"That's true. But only when it comes to food."

He ran his hand through my hair.

I took his hand and kissed it. "What happened to your mother?"

"How do you know something happened to her?"

"You said you didn't have anyone."

He looked away. "She was killed."

"How?"

He poured himself another glass of wine. "She was killed," he said again. "We never found her body. She was a social worker. She was beautiful, my mother. She had me when she was seventeen. She was always young and fierce and so incredibly alive. All the men would always look at her. She became something of an activist. The transvestites made her into one, I think. Not that I blamed her for fighting. And then one day, she didn't come home. She just disappeared."

That was the look he had, the look he wore on his face: the remnants of hurt, the emotional scar, the knowledge that all the laughter in the world could be swept away by a capricious wind at any moment. And there was nothing he could do about it.

There weren't any tears in his eyes. "I looked for her and looked for her and looked for her. The police did nothing. No one did anything. And who was she to them, anyway, just another woman who disappeared into the desert, her flesh swallowed up by the fucking sand." And then his tears came just exactly in the same way that rainstorms came up in the desert, thunder, lightning, angry, monstrous rains that almost felt like bullets. I held him as he sobbed and wondered why the world was so cruel and why good and beautiful and decent men like Javier mattered so little when they should have mattered so much.

"It's not true," I whispered, "that you don't have anyone." I held his face in my hands. "Do you hear me, Javier?"

I made love to him.

And then he made love to me.

No one had ever whispered my name the way he whispered it. I fell asleep to the sound of my name.

When I woke, he was already dressed. It was night. "I have to go to the hospital," he said.

"I'll take you."

"No. It's just a few blocks."

"It's cold," I said. "You didn't bring a coat." I got up and went to the closet. "Here. Put this on."

He didn't argue with me. He took the coat, put it on and kissed me. Then he was gone.

9.

I wanted to call him, but didn't. I'd leave it up to him. If his uncle was dying, he'd be calling his cousins to come into town, taking care of things. He'd always taken care of things. He was that kind of man. There were takers and there were givers and he was a giver. I thought about him, pictured him sitting next to his uncle's bed.

On Tuesday night, he called. It was late, near midnight. "Will you come?"

"I'll be right there." I said. It didn't take me long to get dressed and rush out the door. The hospital was down the street. I walked up to the fifth floor and found the room. He was there, holding his uncle's hand. I moved next to him and placed my hand on his back.

"They didn't come," he whispered. "His sons. They didn't come."

"You're his son," I said.

We sat and listened to his uncle struggling to breathe. The last breaths of the dying are loud and haunting. The body, even in the dying, wants to live, fights greedily for one more breath of air—and damn the pain.

I knew Javier would stand there until his uncle took his last breath. I stood there with him. That was all I could do.

Javier remained an alert and faithful sentry to the last. When the room grew quiet and still, Javier gasped as if he'd felt the stab of a knife. His body shook. Grief was like that—it was an earthquake in the heart. But grief was also a cruel thief that stole away the control you had over your own body.

I kissed Javier's shoulder—though I doubt he was aware that I was even there. I went to get the nurse. I took my time. Javier had more than earned a moment alone with an uncle he so clearly adored.

He never left the room until the funeral home came to collect the body. By then the sun was rising.

I drove him to his uncle's house. We didn't pass many words between us as we drove. When we arrived, I opened the front door and sat Javier down on a chair, Javier who was drunk with sorrow and exhaustion.

"This was where he sat," he said.

I nodded. "Then it's a good place," I said.

I rummaged through the kitchen and put on some coffee.

Javier walked into the kitchen and sat at the table.

"I don't think I want any coffee," he said.

I nodded. "You should get some sleep."

"I don't want to stay here," he said. "It's too sad."

"Get some things," I said.

He nodded.

The drive to my apartment took less than five minutes, but Javier was asleep when we arrived. I helped him up the stairs, his limp and tired body giving out on him. He fell into bed, all his clothes still on. I took off his shoes and let him sleep.

I threw myself on the couch. When I woke up, Javier was across from me, sitting in my reading chair.

He smiled at me.

"What time is it?"

"It's three in the afternoon."

"How long have you been sitting there?"

"I just woke up. I put on some coffee."

I nodded. "I could use some."

He pulled me from the couch and held me.

"I have to go to the funeral home," he said.

"I'll take you."

"No."

"Then take my car."

He nodded.

We showered together.

I watched him shave. I watched him dress. He was graceful and elegant. Even the sadness on his face was mesmerizing. I didn't know how I'd fallen in love with him. I wasn't the falling-in-love kind of man. Some of my friends had suggested that I was disgustingly self-sufficient. I had never thought of myself that way. Perhaps they were right. But watching Javier at that moment, I wanted to need him. I wanted him to be the air I breathed.

I kissed him as he was putting on his shoes. "I'm sorry," I said. "That you lost him."

He nodded. "He was so sick. It's good," he said. "Sometimes death is good."

"Sometimes it is. But it still hurts."

"Hurt comes with the day, Carlos."

"And sometimes so does love," I said.

I saw the look on his face. I understood at that moment that he was in love with me. And I didn't care that I hadn't earned that love and didn't deserve it. I understood that I would take that love and hold on to it for as long as I could. And the thought entered my head that we would be together—and that we might be happy.

10.

The funeral was at the cathedral where his uncle had attended mass for over fifty years. He had married his wife there, had baptized his children there, had marked and measured his life in that sacred building. It did not matter that neither Javier nor I were believers. How could we believe in a church that did not believe in us—either separately or together? Still, that church and its rituals were a part of us. Our bodies—if not our hearts—were familiar with the medieval chants. There was a strange and intimate comfort there.

His uncle's sons sat in the front row next to Javier. They were formal, successful men who lived in other cities. There was something hard about them, but they were civil and respectful. "They're like my aunt," he said. "Even in love, they are loveless." That made me smile.

There were not many people in attendance. Most of the mourners were not mourners at all, but friends of Javier's. They embraced him and comforted him and it was obvious that he was deeply loved.

At the gravesite, Javier sobbed like a boy, unashamed of his tears.

I could feel my heart leaping towards him in the same way that a believer's heart might leap towards the face of God.

II.

Javier and I settled into what might be called a routine. He would come to stay with me every Friday after work. We would go out, watch a movie, hold hands in the dark theater, go out to dinner, come home, make love. Our lives took on the soft and lovely rhythms of a life that was very nearly normal. On Saturdays, we would go to his uncle's house and work on it. He'd inherited the place with no arguments from his male cousins—who neither needed the money nor wanted any of the remnants of their father's life. We both liked working with our hands. We were both men in that kind of way.

On Sunday mornings, I would write. He would read. In the afternoons, we took turns reading our favorite passages from our favorite novels to each other. Javier would talk about the passages with a fierce intelligence that almost always made me smile. He began to understand what that smile meant, though at first he thought I was merely being condescending.

"What is that smile?"

"Nothing. I'm smiling. I'm listening to you and I'm smiling."

"Because my insights aren't intelligent? Because I'm amusing?" There was an edge in his voice.

"That's not what my smile means."

"Explain it."

"No," I said.

Somehow he accepted that. We tried to learn about each other without explaining ourselves too much. We became each other's favorite books. We were obsessed with reading each other.

The winter left, though not without a fight. It seemed to want to stay, but finally gave in to the inevitable. Changes come with difficulty. Even for the seasons. In the spring, I became obsessed with the novel I was writing. Javier would read what I wrote. But there was a rule: no discussing the novel.

One Sunday evening in the middle of the hottest day of July, we were both reading a book. I was reading Bolaño and he was reading the short stories of J.G. Ballard. I was sitting at my reading chair and Javier was lying on the couch.

I put my book down.

"Will you move here, Javier?"

"Here?"

"With me."

"You mean we don't live together?"

"You live in Juárez. Move here."

"I don't have papers. You know that."

"We can start the process. You already have a visa."

"It's to visit. Your country doesn't want me to stay."

"Don't get wise. And what does it matter what this country wants?"

"Countries are bigger than men."

"Fuck countries. I hate all of them. You are the only country I want."

He didn't say anything. But then a smile ran across his face. "You read the newspaper this morning, didn't you, Carlos?"

"The killings are getting worse."

"I'm safe."

"Safe?"

"Safe enough."

"Move here."

He sat up and put his book down. "I can't leave Juárez."

"Why not?"

"You know why not."

"No, I don't."

"What would happen if everybody left?"

"Then the city would die."

"That's right, Carlos."

"But what if you die?"

"I want you to stop reading newspapers."

"I can't do that, Javier."

"Nothing will happen. We can live like this forever."

"Then I'll move to Juárez."

"No."

"Why not?"

"You belong here."

"I belong with you."

He smiled. "You've never said that before."

"I can tell you every day of my life that I love you. I can. It would be true."

"You don't have to tell me what I already know."

"Then I'll move to Juárez."

"No."

"Why?"

"What if something happens to you?"

"What will happen?"

"You know what I'm talking about."

"And you know what I'm talking about."

We wound up yelling at each other. He had never yelled at me. And I had never yelled at him. The only way to end the conversation was by having sex. Afterwards, we lay there in bed and he whispered, "I can't be anymore than I am, Carlos. This is who I am."

I was not his only love and never would be. Perhaps he loved Juárez more than he loved me. But he was right about me. I was not a jealous man. He could love his Juárez. And he could love me too. That was the way it would be.

"We can live this way forever," I said. It was more heaven than I deserved.

12.

The last Friday in August, I called Javier on his cell. "Are you driving?"

"No, I'm waiting for the Consul to finish his lunch meeting."

"When are you off?"

"I won't be off until around seven. It's a late night. The Ambassador is in town. I have to drive him to Chihuahua on Sunday."

"Okay. Then let's meet at the Kentucky Club for a drink after work. My turn to stay at your place."

I knew he was hesitating.

"Javier?"

"Yes, perfect," he said.

Walking across the bridge, I noticed the emptiness. When I was young, the Santa Fe Bridge had been teeming with pedestrians. Avenida Juárez had been packed with vendors and people from El Paso who were more than ready to unwind after a long week. But those days were gone now. The bridge was nearly deserted. I made my way past the soldiers with rifles slung across their backs, soldiers who more closely resembled highschool boys than men. When I walked through the front door of the Kentucky Club, Javier was sitting at the bar.

We touched each other with our eyes.

"Have you been here long?"

"I just got here."

"I ordered a margarita for you."

"I hate margaritas."

"So do I. I thought we'd have one anyway."

That made me laugh.

We took a seat at a table in the corner.

"No one comes here anymore," I said.

We drank our margaritas. He was quiet but I was talkative. I told him stories about how I used to come here as a young man, about how, once, I had been propositioned by an older gringo who was too drunk to talk. "He could never have gotten it up to have sex."

"You must have been very handsome."

"I never gave it much thought."

"Why?"

"Since when is being handsome a virtue?"

Javier studied me. Like he always studied me.

"You know," I said. "I didn't like thinking about what I looked like. I don't think I liked having a body."

"Why?"

"Someone hurt me. When I was a boy."

Javier studied my face. "You didn't deserve that."

"Take me home," I said.

His place was small—a bedroom, a small living room, a kitchen, a bathroom. He had plants and books everywhere. There were photographs on the walls. And a picture of me in his bedroom. There was a kind of stark elegance to his apartment that reminded me of his smile.

We didn't make love. We just held each other.

I woke in the middle of the night and undressed. Javier was in the next room reading one of my novels.

"Why are you doing that?" I said.

"I'm in love with the author. Did I tell you?"

We didn't sleep the rest of the night.

We made love like boys who had just discovered the wonders of sex.

The next day, we had breakfast with the two women who lived next door. Magda and Sofia. They were schoolteachers and activists and they spoke with sadness about what was happening in their beloved Juárez. I found it strange and illogical and moving that these lovely people could be so faithful to a city that had not earned their love. But they were happy and loved working with children who had next to nothing. I promised to bring them some children's books. "Will you read to them?"

"Yes," I said.

They both smiled at me. "So you are Javier's Carlos."

"Yes. I am Javier's Carlos."

We spent the afternoon reading to each other. In the evening, he walked me to the bridge. I wanted to kiss him. But that was impossible. He hugged me. We might have been old friends.

He promised to call me when he got back from Chihuahua.

On Tuesday evening, he called.

On Wednesday, he texted me: *Te adoro.*

I texted him back: *See you on Friday.*

He texted me back: *Take me to a movie.*

On Friday, I waited for him. He never came.

14.

I kept calling his cell phone, but it had been turned off. I paced my apartment,

trying to remember the last time I talked to him. I tried not to panic. I had

the number to the embassy but it would be closed. It was no use to call them.

I walked across the street to the corner grocery store and bought a pack of

cigarettes. The first one tasted like a pigeon had shit in my mouth. But I didn't

care. I smoked another. I poured myself a drink.

I didn't sleep all night. I kept running different scenarios through my

head. I was, after all, a writer. Maybe he was having an affair with another

man. Unimaginative as that scenario was, I insisted upon it. Because it meant

Javier was alive.

By six o'clock, I was knocking at Magda and Sofia's door. By the look on

their faces, I knew they weren't surprised to see me.

"You look terrible," Magda said as she pushed me toward the couch.

Sofia went into the kitchen and came out with a cup of coffee. She

offered me a cigarette. I took it. I listened to my own lungs take in the smoke.

"Tell me what happened to Javier?"

"We didn't have your number. We didn't know how to contact you."

"What happened?"

"Thursday night—," Sofia looked at Magda.

Magda nodded at her.

"They came."

"Who?"

"Some men. They had rifles. Or maybe not rifles. Weapons. We heard them. It wasn't dark yet. They were dragging Javier out into the street. They were rounding up all the men from the neighborhood. They must have been looking for someone in particular. So they took them all."

Magda lit a cigarette. "She wanted to stop them, but I didn't let her out of the house."

I nodded and looked at Sofia. "You're a lion. But they would have killed you."

"Maybe they haven't killed anyone."

"You believe that?"

Magda looked down at the floor. "They were looking for someone else. It was all a mistake."

"Do they let their mistakes live?"

15.

I drove to the U.S. Consulate. They were closed on weekends but there was always someone there. I managed to get the attention of one of the chauffeur's who was sitting in a car inside the gate. "I'm a friend of Javier's," I yelled.

He walked to the gate. I introduced myself. He gave me his name. Manuel. He shook my hand. "Javier reads your books," he said.

I nodded.

I told him what Magda and Sofia had told me.

He shook his head.

He let me in. I sat alone in a waiting room. Manuel walked back into the room and asked me for my cell phone number. He walked out of the room. A few minutes later, I got a call from a man named Neil who worked at the consulate. "Manuel told me what happened to Javier. Can you tell me the story again?" So I told him. "Oh no," he said. I could tell he had some respect if not some affection for Javier. He told me they would do what they could to find out what happened to Javier. I don't think he was lying. But they would find out nothing.

The consulate never received any information regarding Javier's disappearance. And if they did, they did not share it with me.

For a week, all I did was search. I spoke to Javier's neighbors. No one said anything. Everyone was afraid. Some of them had lost their own men in that raid. Their sons. Their fathers. One woman told me to go back to El Paso. *Y no vuelvas. Nadie sabe nada. Y si saben no te van a decir.* She was right. No one was going to tell me anything.

I went to the police.

The police told me that they'd received a phone call from the consulate and that they were looking for Javier. "He's probably just running away from his wife and his responsibilities." That's what I was told. I didn't bother to tell him that I was as close to a wife as Javier would ever have.

I went to the newspapers.

I talked to lawyers.

I talked to human rights activists.

I talked to my congressman.

No one really wanted to talk to me. I began to understand what it feels like to be invisible.

I thought of looking in the desert, but where in the desert would I look?

He was gone. Javier. And I knew I would never see him again. I was angry at my own heart that refused to give up hope despite the fact that I begged it to give up. I began spending weekends in Javier's small apartment. Magda and

Sofia told me that I was putting myself in danger. "I don't care," I said. "They can take me too."

I would call the consulate three or four times a week.

I would visit the police station and ask questions.

I kept talking to reporters.

I would sleep in Javier's bed and dream him back to life. The dreams were all the same. He was happy and reading a book. He was touching me. He was making love to me. We were walking down Avenida Juárez holding hands. I would wake to his books and to his plants. I always called his name and waited for him to answer.

I never cried. There was nothing but the numbness of my angry heart.

I stopped calling the consulate.

I stopped calling the police.

Months passed. I stopped writing.

And then I stopped going to Javier's apartment. I just stopped. It had been months. Winter had returned.

One evening in December I got a phone call from Magda. "Come," she said.

I felt something in my heart. "Have they found him?"

"No," she said. "You have to stop hoping."

I nodded into the receiver.

"Sofia and I have something for you."

I walked from my apartment to the bridge. I took a cab to Sofia and Magda's house. Sofia offered me a glass of wine.

I took the glass. Magda offered me a cigarette. "No," I said. "It doesn't help."

"I'm happy you loved him so much."

"I'm not," I said. "What does love do except make you sad?"

"Without it, we would be even sadder."

Sofia took something out from her purse. I could see what it was. Javier's watch. The watch his father had given him. He never took it off.

"Where did you find it?"

"Some people talked to us."

"Who? Who talked to you? Who?"

"It doesn't matter who, Carlos."

"It does matter."

"You have to leave this alone, Carlos."

"Why?"

"You know why."

I nodded.

"They led us to where he was."

"You should have taken me."

"We went at night. It wasn't safe."

"So he's—"

"He has gone to be with the women. With all the nameless women who have been buried in the desert."

I nodded and thought, *He has gone to be with his mother.*

She handed me the watch.

I found that I was kissing it. How banal. To sit and kiss a lover's watch.

16.

I don't remember leaving Magda and Sofia's house.

I vaguely remember walking down some half-familiar streets.

I walked for a long time.

I found myself sitting at the bar in the Kentucky Club.

I had a drink and then another—and then another.

I stared at Javier's watch.

I don't know how long I sat there at the bar, drinking, trying not to think. Trying not to hate. Trying not to feel anything.

And then I just wanted to go home. But where was home?

THE ART OF TRANSLATION

There were moments when I sensed my mother and father at my side, staring at me as if they were trying to sift through the wreckage of a storm, trying to find my remains. My mother would touch me, hold my hand, whisper words to me, words I couldn't understand. I felt as if I was no longer in control of my own voice, my own body. When my mother looked into my eyes and kissed my forehead, I stared back into her almost familiar face. I could see the hurt in her eyes as she whispered my name and I felt as if I had become a wound, the source of all her hurt.

My brothers and sisters came to visit. I looked at all of them as though they were perfect strangers. I stared into their eyes, listened to their voices. I felt as if they must have all been hiding somewhere in my memory. I would look at my fingers and whisper their names and count them when I was lying in bed in the dark: *Cecilia, Angela, Monica, Alfredo, Ricardo. One, two, three, four, five.* And then I would repeat the names again and again and again. And count *one, two, three, four, five.* I must have loved them once, and I tried to remember that love but there was nothing there. Only their names remained and their expectant faces. Angela kept repeating, *How could they have done this? How could they do this to you?* But didn't she know? She was eight years older. How could she not know how cruel the world was? No, not the world, the world was neither cruel nor kind. But the boys in the world—it was the boys that were cruel—that's how they translated the world, with fists, with rage, with violence. And what good did it do to think about all these things, to ask why when there was no answer?

And wasn't their last name Guerra? And didn't that name mean war? And didn't that mean that they were born to fight? But being born to fight did not mean that they were born to win the battles they fought. As I repeated the names of my brothers and sisters and felt each syllable on my tongue, I wondered what their names meant and wondered if they had scars too, scars that they were hiding from me and hiding from my mom and dad and from the world. And wasn't that the way it should be? Shouldn't everyone's scars be silent and hidden? Shouldn't we all pretend perfection and beauty and the optimism of a perfect day in spring? Why not? This was America, the country of happiness, and we had come from Mexico, the most tragic country in the world. And the only thing me—and those like me—were allowed to feel was gratitude. The boys who had hurt me, they spoke a different language and it was not a language I understood and maybe never would understand.

My brothers and sisters came in the evenings, all of them, as I lay in the hospital room. And I was trying, really trying, and I spoke to them softly but I wasn't really aware of the words I was speaking and what did it matter if what I was saying didn't mean anything at all? I felt as if it was someone else who was uttering words in an unknown language. And they were kind, my brothers and sisters, so kind, and they said I was looking better and I was surprised that I understood what they were saying. I smiled and squeezed their hands when they squeezed mine and I wondered what they felt because all I felt was that I was left for dead on the outskirts of Albuquerque on a warm night when I had stepped out to mail a letter. That was all I was doing, mailing a letter at the post office and then I heard someone yelling names at me and then I was being dragged away and kicked and everything changed. And here I was in a hospital room, not dead, *not dead*. But I knew that something in me had died. I did not know the name for that something.

I felt like an impersonator. I found it disconcerting that everyone still remembered who I was. But I knew that whoever it was they remembered was gone and I did not believe that the boy they had loved would ever come back.

I looked at my father and touched his face as if I were a boy who was staring at a man for the first time in his life. There was something sad about my father's face, and yet there was something hard and angry about it too. It seemed to me that the hospital room was suffering from a chronic silence. It was as though all sound had been banished from the world and the words and the laughter had been sent back to Mexico and I had been forced to stay in this foreign land that hated me. That's what they had said when I'd felt the knife slicing into my back *Why don't you go back to where you came from? Motherfucker, motherfucker, go back, go back.* But not knowing my way back, I was forced to stay.

The doctor asked me if I knew my name.

I looked back at the doctor. I was trying to decide if he was real or if he was just a dream I was having.

The doctor looked back at me, stubbornly waiting for an answer.

I didn't want to talk to him. But I decided he wasn't a dream and that he wasn't going to go away. "Yes," I said, "I know my name."

"You want to tell me what it is?"

"Don't you know?"

"Can you just tell me?"

"My name is Nick."

"What's your last name?"

"Guerra."

"What year is it?"

I decided the doctor wasn't a bad man. He wasn't like the boys. He wasn't going to hurt me. I think I might have smiled at him.

"What year is it, Nick?"

"1985."

The doctor nodded and smiled and I wondered if he had a son.

"Who's the president?"

I closed my eyes. "Ronald Reagan."

"Who's the vice president?"

"Bush? Is it Bush? Does it matter?"

The doctor smiled. "You've suffered quite a shock, Nick."

"Is that what it was?"

The doctor touched my shoulder and I flinched, a reflex. "Steady," the doctor whispered. "No one's going to hurt you here." His smile was kind and it almost made me want to cry. "You're going to be just fine, Nick."

I wanted to believe him. I shut my eyes. I wanted to sleep.

When I woke in the darkness of the hospital room, I thought I heard the sound of my own voice. A nurse rushed into the room. I looked at her with a question on my face. "You were screaming," she said.

"Oh," I said. "I'm thirsty."

She gave me a glass of water.

"I'm sorry they did this to you," she said.

"You're sure I was screaming?"

"Yes."

"I was dreaming," I said. "It rhymes with screaming."

"What do you remember, Nick?" It was the doctor again. It wasn't night anymore and I was glad.

"Do you remember being transferred here from the hospital in Albuquerque?"

"Albuquerque?" I whispered. "Is that an English word?"

The doctor had a puzzled look on his face. "No, I don't think it is."

"What does it mean?"

"I don't know, Nick."

He was quiet for a moment. His eyes were green and silent and I didn't know what his silence meant.

"Nick, do you remember arriving here?"

"No."

"What do you remember?"

"Why does it matter?"

"Do you know what city you're in?"

"Home."

"Home?"

"El Paso."

"Is that a guess?"

I shook my head. "When will you let me out of here?"

"I'm worried about you, Nick."

"I thought you said I was going to be fine."

When the doctor left, I wondered what the word for worry was in Spanish. I couldn't think of the word. It was gone. In order to translate words from one language to another, you had to know both languages. The languages I knew were disappearing. I wondered if I would have to find a way to live without words.

When my mother told me I was being released, I smiled at her.

"We're taking you home," she said.

I nodded.

"Why won't you talk, Nick?"

"I talk," I said.

"You don't."

I remember the trip back to my old neighborhood, the familiar houses. It was as if I was watching myself get down from the car, watching myself as I stared at my father's neat and perfect lawn. My mother's roses were in bloom and I thought they were very beautiful and I spelled out the word *beautiful* to myself and I wondered about the origins of that word and what kind of dreamer had dragged it into the world.

I wandered the rooms of the house. Nothing seemed foreign. But nothing seemed familiar. I stared at the pictures on the wall. There was a picture of me as a boy and I held an Easter basket and my sister Angela was kissing me.

I wanted to sleep. I was tired.

The bandages on my back were gone. I wondered if the words they wrote on my skin had disappeared—but I knew they were still there. They would always be there. And then I laughed to myself. What if they had misspelled the words?

The newspapers started calling almost immediately after I was released from the hospital. How did they know I was home? I watched my parents as they struggled to answer everyone's hungry questions. *No, they couldn't speak to me, yes, it was outrageous, no, the family had no comment, please, please, no, no, describe how you feel. Describe how you feel?*

I didn't like that my mother and father hovered over me as if I was a bird born with a broken wing.

I noticed how my mother would flinch every time the phone rang. A reporter from one of the TV stations showed up at our front door, cameraman in tow, and smiled sympathetically at my mother as she stood at the door. "We'd like to feature you," she said. "Would you mind saying something, just a short interview? Actually, would the boy like to say something?"

"His name is Nick," my mother said stiffly. "And he's a man, *not* a boy." She shut the door. I studied the look on her face. I thought she was going to cry—but she didn't and I was glad she didn't because I didn't know how to calm her. I could see her lips trembling and I knew it was because of me. When the reporter began taping her segment using our house as a background, I stood in quiet awe of my sister Angela who stormed out into the yard, grabbed the reporter's microphone, looked into the camera and yelled: "Someone used my brother's back like a goddamned chalkboard. You want to know what they wrote on his back? Is that what you want? You want to know how we feel? We fucking feel like dancing." She tossed the microphone into the neighbor's yard and stared at them until they drove away.

I watched her from the doorway. I wondered how it was that she came to be the owner of that rage. I wanted it for myself but there was nothing in me. I was a tree who had lost its leaves in the middle of spring. When Angela came back into the house, she was shaking. I put my hand on her back and felt the sobs washing through her body. I wanted to beg her to give me her tears.

A magazine from Chicago called. Would it be possible to interview me over the phone. "No," my mother said. The reporter pushed, wanting to know how I was doing. Would I be permanently scarred? Was I returning to college in the fall? Did I hate the boys who'd done this? What did I think about the Hispanic community's reaction? Did I support the student demonstrators? My mother listened patiently to all her questions—then hung up the phone.

The phone calls became routine—calls from friends, from acquaintances, from people we didn't know, most of them offering sympathy. I asked myself if sympathy was a good word or a bad word. But there were other phone calls too, calls that were not related to the word sympathy. *Wasn't it true that the boy had done something to those other boys? He must have provoked them, goaded them into attacking him. Surely the boys must have had a reason. Couldn't it be true that the boy wanted to start some kind of race war? Did the boy have papers? What was an illegal doing at a public university?*

I looked up the word *illegal*.

An anonymous caller said that I was lucky. "They didn't exactly lynch him, did they?"

My father had our phone number changed.

But even after that, when the phone rang, my parents gave each other tentative glances before they answered it.

Everything felt like it was happening to someone else. The newspaper people and the journalists, they didn't want to speak to me. They wanted to speak to a Nick who no longer existed. The dead couldn't speak. Didn't they know that? The thought occurred to me that the living were exhausted from the weight of the words they were forced to carry with them everywhere they went.

I at least felt free of the weight of words. *Why don't you talk, Nick?*

If I lay still in my bed, maybe I would dissolve like dry ice in a glass of water. To melt, to turn into a gas, to float away. To disappear.

But my mother's food—and the smell of it—reminded me that having a body wasn't always a bad thing. The odor of her *sopas* and *caldillos* and *guisados*. The garlic, the onion, the cumin, the cilantro, the roasted chiles. Sometimes, the odors that came out of my mother's kitchen made me want to live.

Taste lies on the tongue but it is beyond the reach of language. That's what I wrote down on a piece of paper. I stared at what I had written. I ripped up the piece of paper until all the words were indecipherable.

My mother came into my room one night. She sat on my bed. "I thought you'd be reading," she said.

"I don't want to read anymore."

"You told me you couldn't live without books. You said you wanted to learn all the meanings of every word that existed in the world."

"I don't remember saying that. It must have been a long time ago."

"No, Nick, it wasn't long ago at all."

"I don't feel that way anymore."

"What were you thinking about?"

"What?"

She kissed my forehead. "When I walked in the room, Nick, you were thinking about something."

"My scars." I didn't know why I said that.

"They're not just places of hurt, Nick. They're places of healing." My mother and I disagreed about how to translate the words on my back.

I felt the soundless tears running down my face.

I let her rock me to sleep.

I woke to the sound of thunder. I'd been having the same dream, the white sun beating down on me, the blood on my back as purple as Lenten vestments. But the morning storm was stronger than the dream. I opened my eyes, heard the drops pounding the house, smelled the pungent odor of the thirsty creosote.

I ran my hands under my T-shirt, feeling my own smooth chest. I caught myself reaching for the scars on my back, the tough, raised skin. I rose from my bed and stared out the window. I watched as my father's peach trees swayed to the rhythm of the wind and the water.

Days, weeks, months of nothing but sun.

The learning to live without water.

The parched land.

The waiting.

And then the rain.

When I was a child, the whole world stopped at the sound of the thunder. I had a memory of people stepping out of their houses. The people would watch and listen closely as if each drop that fell to the ground was a whisper of a loved one come back from the dead.

I tried to picture my brothers and sisters playing outside, their laughter distant and lost amid the thunder, their bodies glowing in the bolts of lightning. I saw myself running toward them. Together, me, my brothers and sisters, all of us laughing, happy, together.

The storm stopped as suddenly as it began. The image of my brothers and sisters disappeared. I looked up at the immaculate, clearing sky.

I moved away from the window, then sat on my bed. I decided to go for a run. I was sick of feeling the presence of three white boys that had occupied my body. Their hate sat inside me like a bird who was nesting—waiting for her eggs to hatch. I decided I could get used to hating, could even learn to love it in the same way that I'd learned to love the desert.

You could learn to love anything.

I yawned, stretched my arms upwards and left them reaching towards the sky until they hurt. I looked in the closet for my running shoes and found that all of my shoes were neatly arranged. My mother must have unpacked and organized everything. She was good at turning chaos into order.

I grabbed my running shoes, opened a drawer and found a pair of socks. I changed into my running clothes, then walked into the kitchen. My mother and father were drinking coffee and reading the newspaper. They looked up at me carefully—as if they were afraid I might break if they said the wrong thing. A part of me wanted to laugh, but the other part had forgotten how to laugh.

"Hi," I said.

I thought I saw something in my mother's eyes. She was either happy or sad—I couldn't decide.

"I'm going running," I said.

"Be careful," my mother said. "You're still a little weak."

"Just a short run, Mom."

"You want breakfast when you come back?"

"Sounds nice." I looked at my father. "You were right, Dad."

"About what?"

"You said I should have stayed home and gone to college here. You were right."

He didn't say anything. He ran his fingers through his thick, graying hair. "It doesn't matter. You're going to be okay. You're home now."

I nodded and kissed my father on the top of his head as I walked out the door. I wondered why I had done that but it seemed like the right thing to do. The old Nick would have done that. *You're home now.* Home. I thought that word was just a dream.

I half expected the ground to give, open up and swallow me whole. But every time I took a step, nothing happened. I found myself heading toward the desert, but as I reached it, I stopped as if I had reached a line I was not allowed to cross. I looked toward the houses behind me, all in neat rows, all with numbers and mailboxes and sidewalks. I wondered why people had such a need to make the desert into something tame. Green lawns and flowers. It was all so futile—and such a waste of water. I sat down and looked at the well-trimmed hedges, the flowers struggling to survive.

I walked past all the homes and stood at the edge of the desert. I looked out at the mesquites and chamizos and the cacti. They always caught me there in the dream, caught me in the desert. They lived there, those boys, the three of them, the white boys who had hurt me. They lived in all the deserts of the earth. Death. That was the new word for desert. So that's where they lived now, in every desert, in every dream I would ever have. I knew they would find me someday, catch me, cut me up again. I turned my back on the desert I once loved and ran home.

Breakfast was waiting for me when I walked into the house. "I'm out of shape." I smiled at my mother. "Smells good."

"*Huevos con chorizo.*"

I washed my hands at the sink.

My mother pushed the plate in front of me. "You're too thin."

I nodded, began eating, then looked around the room. "When did you paint the kitchen?"

"Two weeks ago."

"Guess I haven't been much help around here."

"You're looking better, *mijo. Y no se te quita lo bonito.*"

"Mom, I'm plain as a row of cotton."

"A row of cotton is anything but plain."

"You want me to argue with you, Mom?"

"It would make me feel better if you did."

I shrugged, took a tortilla and scooped my eggs up into my mouth. "Good," I said. "This is really good."

My mom looked almost happy. "What are you going to do now, Nick?"

I forced a smile as I looked into my father's dark eyes. I thought they looked like a winter night. "Now? Today?"

"Yes. Now."

"Now?"

"Now that you're alive again."

"Oh," I said. "So that's it. I'm alive?" I rolled my eyes.

"See, you always did that before—" She took a drink from her cup of coffee. "You always used to do that. You're home now, Nick. You're home."

I looked up the old words in the dictionary, words I'd once known the meanings of: *home, desert, death, knife, skin, blood, knife, hate.*

Waiting tables is not what I had dreamed of doing. Not that I minded the job. Café Central. My oldest brother knew the owner. It was the nicest restaurant in the city. The food was as good as it was expensive. And the money was even better than the food. Not that I gave a damn. What was I going to do with the money?

I liked my new routine. Running in the morning, going to work in the evening. It almost didn't matter that nothing happened in between.

Sometimes, I wanted to go out after work. Going out sounded like something normal. I wanted normal, but something about normal scared me. Walking down streets at night. Something bad would happen. But there was this bar that all the waiters talked about, some dive called the Regal Beagle. I wanted to go. Normal.

One Saturday, I made up my mind. The bar was walking distance from the restaurant—but I decided to drive. I parked half a block away. I walked into the bar and smiled nervously as I looked around. I sat on a stool and ordered a drink. I polished off my bourbon in three gulps. I ordered another. As I finished my second drink, I thought about having a third—but already I felt lightheaded.

I didn't notice her sitting next to me—until she spoke. "What's your name?" Her voice was deep and raspy as if she had a cold. I stared at her cigarette, the smoke coming out of her mouth. "I'm Sylvia."

I nodded.

"Quiet, huh?"

"Not much to say."

"So what's your name?" She smiled. She was pretty when she smiled. I guessed she was in her thirties—maybe older. It was hard to tell in the dim light of the bar.

"Nicholas," I said. "My name is Nicholas." I tried to pretend it was normal for me to be sitting in a dark bar having a couple of drinks and talking to a woman. Men did it all the time. Normal.

"You look nervous." She offered me a cigarette.

"I don't smoke."

She laughed. "Maybe you should."

"No thanks." I caught the bartender's eyes, lifted my glass.

"Aren't you going to offer me one too?"

I smiled. "Sure." Men sat at bars and bought women drinks all the time. Normal. I caught the bartender's eye and tapped her glass.

The bartender placed a beer in front of her. "He's a little young for you, isn't he, Sylvia?"

She laughed, then she looked at me. "Are you too young?"

"I'm old enough to drink," I said.

"Well, if you're old enough to drink." She laughed.

"You laugh a lot."

"Well, there's a lot to laugh about." She took a sip of her beer.

"So what kind of beer do you drink?"

"Bud."

I watched her lips move as she talked. I liked the sound of her voice—what she was saying didn't matter so much. And anyway, men weren't good at translating what women said. Something about her job and her ex-husband. We had another drink. I felt strange, like I was someone else. I wanted to know what it was like to kiss her, thought I'd like to try. But it didn't seem right. "I better go," I said. "It's late."

"We're just getting started."

"Are we?"

"What do you say we go to Juárez?"

I thought a moment. I'd already had too much to drink and then I heard myself saying, "What the fuck."

She laughed. "Yeah, what the fuck."

She held my hand as we walked over the Santa Fe Bridge. I found myself sitting at a booth in the Kentucky Club. It was strange. I should have felt drunker than I felt. She asked me questions. I answered them and I smiled to myself because I knew the answers weren't true. Men lied to women all the time. *Normal.*

We weren't there long. She said she liked the Florida better. So we walked down the street and had another drink. Maybe two. It was late and I was tired but she was kissing me as we sat there and I was kissing her back. "We should go," I said.

"Where to?" She was smiling. "My place? Your place?"

"Your place," I said.

She was still smiling. "I don't live so far."

She must have seen something in my expression.

"You don't have to be so shy."

"It's the way I am."

When I took her hand, I thought that it was as warm as the night. I could feel myself trembling.

"I won't hurt you," she said.

Her apartment was small and bare--but it was clean. She offered me a beer. I told her I should go, didn't know what I was doing there, but when she reached over and kissed me again, I kissed her back and didn't want to stop. It was strange, her tongue, the taste of cigarette and beer, but it was sweet, and I wanted to tell her I'd never done this before but words didn't matter. They had never mattered. She unbuttoned my shirt, laughed because I was wearing a T-shirt underneath, and when my shirt was off, she tried to take off my T-shirt. I stopped her. "Not my T-shirt." I hadn't meant to sound angry, but that's the way it came out. She looked at me, said everything was okay. "Then how about your pants?" I kissed her again, then let her take off my pants, then my underwear. I felt her warm hands on my legs, on my penis. I groaned softly.

"Nice," she said. She stood in front of me and took off her clothes. I reached over and felt her body. I pulled her close to me and when I felt her back, it was smooth and unscarred.

"What do you like?" she asked.

"Just don't touch my back."

I woke to the sound of her breathing. I felt still and serene, and yet I felt worn out and hungover. I'd never woken up in someone else's bed. In the dim light of the lamp, I could make out her features, the wrinkles around her eyes. She was forty—at least forty, maybe older. But she had felt young when I was inside her, and I had felt something I had no name for—and there hadn't been any dreams. When we had been having sex, I had almost felt happy to be the owner of a body, happy, and I'd liked that moment of almost happiness. I had liked it so much.

I wondered if I'd pleased her. Maybe I hadn't. Maybe she didn't care. I lay there, the steady rhythm of her breathing like a lullaby. I felt stupid and guilty. But she hadn't cared. She was used to this, had placed the condom on me as if it was just another simple and ordinary task—like drinking a glass of water. I stared at the white of my T-shirt, wondered if her smell would be on it when I went back home.

I looked at my watch. Three o'clock in the morning, and I was lying in a stranger's bed. I wanted to leave, but I liked looking at her in the dim light of the lamp on her nightstand. I just kept staring. Suddenly I wondered if I owed her any money. It had all been too easy. Why would anybody want to sleep with me if it wasn't for money? I sat up on the bed. My clothes were in the other room. I heard her voice.

"Going home, Mr. T-shirt?"

I turned around and looked at her. "Yeah," I said. "Gotta get some sleep and go to work. Do I owe—"

"I'm not a fucking prostitute."

"Sorry," I said. "I just thought that—"

"Doesn't matter."

"It does matter. Look, I don't do—I mean why would anybody want to sleep—I mean—"

"You don't get out much."

"No, I don't."

"I could tell."

"That bad, huh?"

"No. You're nice. Last night was nice."

"And I'm young enough to be your son."

"So what? What's wrong with sleeping with someone you want to sleep with?"

"Nothing."

"Well, then?"

"You're not mad?"

"Go home. I bet you live with your parents."

"So what?"

"Don't get mad."

"I gotta go."

"Want my phone number?"

I got up from the bed. I didn't like feeling stupid. So stupid. I walked into the living room, put on my pants, then carried my shoes and socks back into the bedroom. I sat on the bed and put on my shoes and socks. "Yeah," I whispered.

"Yeah what?"

"Yeah, I want your phone number."

"Good boy. Next time can I see your back?"

"No."

"What's wrong with it?"

"Nothing."

"Nothing?"

"I don't like to talk about it."

"Talking never hurt anybody."

"Look, it's private."

"So's your dick."

"Forget it, then." I put on my shoes, then stood up. "I'm sorry. I'm being an asshole. But that's the way it is with me."

"Fuck you," she said.

"Yeah, right." I slammed the door on my way out.

I looked up more words: *sex, kiss, hands, tongue*. No dictionary could define, could translate, the needs of the human body. I looked up the name *Sylvia*. It was Latin for forest. Maybe it was a place I could get lost in.

A week later, I found her at the Regal Beagle again, smoking her cigarette, drinking her beer. I wanted to apologize. I wanted to explain to her about my back. But I'd never spoken to anyone about what happened, not to my brothers and sisters, not to my parents, not to anyone. Well, except for the police—but that didn't count.

I sat next to her at the bar. "I'm sorry," I said.

She smiled.

I went home with her. Our sex was angry—more like a fight than sex. And even though there was plenty of life in the sex, there was no love. There was no love at all. Not that I was surprised. When I fell asleep, I woke up as she was trying to take off my T-shirt.

"I fucking said no," I said.

"Just get out!" she yelled. "Just get the fuck out! You're a fucked-up kid."

I didn't say a word as I finished putting on my clothes. She *was* right. I was fucked up.

"You're fucked up," she said again.

"I heard you the first time."

I felt a sharp pain on my back as I moved toward the door. I tried not to wince, tried not to show any sign of pain as I started at the glass ashtray that had bounced off my back and had fallen to the floor with a thud. "Who's more fucked up—me or you?"

"Is it a contest?" The look on her face, it reminded me of the look on the faces of those boys, the rage in it, the hate.

I took a deep breath and walked out the door.

I thought my back would have another bruise by the time I woke up in the morning. I started the engine, then sat in the idling car for a long time. Finally, I put the car in drive. As I drove home in the morning light, I found myself repeating basic Spanish grammar: *yo soy, tu eres, el es, nosotros somos, ustedes son, ellos son*. I whispered the word for the sun, *sol*, then whispered the word for night, *noche*. I liked night better than sun. Y*o soy una noche sin estrellas*.

It was a sentence. A real sentence. The words did not feel foreign on my tongue.

As I lay in bed, words from my youth came back to me. *Fuego. Lluvia. Desierto. Coraje. Odio. Trabajo. Sangre. Corazón. Muerte.* I repeated the words to myself, used each one in a simple sentence, then translated it to myself: *Tengo la sangre de mi hermana.* I have my sister's blood. *En el desierto no cae lluvia.* Rain does not fall in the desert. *Tengo odio en mi corazón.* I have hate in my heart. I wondered if my translations were accurate. I fell asleep translating, trying to make sense of what was inside me — but how could I translate the words on my back? How could I translate what had happened?

I woke up in the afternoon.

I went for a run in the desert.

The boys were there. They would always be there. They would be everywhere I went. There was nothing to do but outrun them. But their hate was a bullet. And who could outrun a bullet?

When I got back home, I took a shower. I knew that nothing could wash away the scars. I looked at myself in the mirror. My eyes were as black as a starless night.

My mother asked me if I was okay.

I nodded.

"You don't look okay."

"It's just a hangover," I said.

"You never used to drink," she said.

There's a lot of things I never used to do. That's what I wanted to say. But I didn't bother. I understood that my mom felt the presence of those words in the room.

I went to work. I waited tables.

I came home and went to my room and prayed for sleep. I remembered me as a boy, leaning into my mother's shoulder during mass and wondering if God saw us. I remembered watching my father work in the sun, his skin glowing in his own sweat. I remembered the boy I had been in high school, looking up words in a dictionary. I fell asleep trying to think of the word for what I felt.

When I woke in the morning, I told myself that the scars on my back had always been there. They were nothing more than birthmarks. I thought of that night. I told myself I should *not* have yelled; I should *not* have been outraged as if that act had been undeserved and violent and indecent; I should *not* have begged them to stop in the name of a god I did not even believe in. What I should have done—when they were holding me down— what I should have done when they took that knife and wrote on me as if the knife was merely a pen and my own blood nothing more than ink—what I should have done—I should have looked at my attackers and told them I had been waiting for them. I should have looked them all in the eyes and told them I knew their hate, understood it, embraced its awful necessity. I should have offered up my body as a sacrifice to their cruel and hungry gods. It was a war, after all, and sacrifices were necessary in a war—though I had never acknowledged that the war existed.

War. *Guerra.* That was me. That was my name.

And then I knew that I would have to relearn the meaning of every word I had ever learned. I would have to learn how to translate all those words. Thousands of them. Millions of them. And then I smiled and felt the tears running down my face. Finally I understood. It wasn't the words that mattered. *It was me. I mattered.* So now I would have to fight to translate myself back into the world of the living.

THE RULE MAKER

I.

There are things I still remember about growing up in Juárez: I remember
the name of my school, Escuela Carlos Amaya. I remember my first grade
teacher's name, Laura Cedillos. I wanted her to be my mother, not because
she was pretty, but because she was so nice and smelled like flowers. I
remember the playground, cement and dirt and grass that never really grew
up to become a lawn because it was never watered and because we stomped
the ground until it was a fine powder. We couldn't pound anything else but we
could pound the dirt.

I remember the fence around the school, a fence that was there to make
us feel safe. I remember the first time I got into a fight. I wasn't any good at
it. I was eight and Marcos Manriquez punched me right in the stomach and I
writhed on the ground in pain. "*¡Levantate!*" he screamed. But I just lay there
on the ground and refused to get up. Everyone laughed at me and called me
a *joto* and all the other mean names kids call each other. I don't think I cared
that they called me names. It didn't bother me because I didn't think it was
a good thing to know how to fight, to use your fists on other people. I never

liked the idea of hurting other people—and if that made me a *joto,* then I
guess that's what I was. Not that I knew what *joto* meant at the time.

And anyway, after that fight, Marcos and I became friends. Marcos had
good fists. But he had a better heart. He was the best friend I ever had. We
rode our bikes around the streets of my neighborhood yelling and screaming
and laughing. And then one day my bike got stolen.

I never really knew where my mother got the money for us to live.
We had an okay house, small, two bedrooms, a living room, a bathroom,
a kitchen. The walls were all painted white—except the yellow and blue
kitchen. My mother had a picture of San Martín Caballero in her kitchen. San
Martín was a gentleman on a horse and he was offering a beggar his cloak. I
don't know why I remember that. I guess you could say he became my patron
saint because I've always given beggars on the streets all the change in my
pockets. I didn't have a cloak like San Martín Caballero, but I always had a
quarter and a few pennies.

The small house where I grew up was clean—but it was clean because
I taught myself how to clean a house. It's not a bad thing to teach yourself
things. And besides, I didn't want the house I lived in to be dirty and I
didn't want the house to smell bad. I sometimes sprayed the house with my
mother's perfume. Except my room. I didn't spray my room with anything.
It smelled like old books and it probably smelled like me. Maybe my room
didn't smell so good, but I took a shower every day and I always brushed my
teeth and combed my hair. And I washed my own clothes.

There wasn't a father in the house. I didn't know if my mother had
been married or not married and nobody ever said anything about him. I
remember asking her once, "Do you have a picture of my father?"

She looked right at me and said, *"Nunca quiero que me preguntes de tu papá.*" I knew it was serious business because she almost always spoke to me in English. When she spoke to me in Spanish, it meant I'd better listen. She had this thing that I had to learn English, even though I lived in Juárez. She said I was a U.S. citizen and that I should know the language of my country. But Juárez was the only country I knew—and it was the only country I cared about. She'd bring me to El Paso sometimes and I'd play with my cousins and we spoke both languages, English and Spanish. But El Paso wasn't Juárez and it wasn't mine and I always felt that I was just a visitor there.

I had a friend named Jorge who lived next door. I liked Jorge's family because even though my mother disappeared for days, they always watched out for me. And Jorge's dad was good to me and he would take me and Jorge with him to do things and I sometimes felt like he was my dad—only I knew he wasn't. I was sad sometimes, but not sad, sad, sad. Just sad in a normal way, I think.

I liked my life when I lived in Juárez. And even though I was sad sometimes, I was also happy sometimes. I loved my mother and it's not as if she was really mean to me. I knew she had lots of problems. People can't help it when they have problems. Everyone in the world has problems—even rich people. At least that's what Jorge's father said. Jorge's mother said that maybe it was true that rich people had problems too. But she also said, "If the rich don't care about the problems of the poor, then why should the poor care about the problems of the rich?"

The rich and the poor, they were big topics of conversation in Jorge's house. In my house too.

2.

My mother never hit me, not once, not ever, and she kissed me just when I needed to be kissed. She would read books to me in English and I liked listening to her voice. I asked her where she had learned to read and speak in English. She said her mother had sent her to Loretto High School in El Paso. It was a good school, a Catholic girls' school. "Those were the best days," she said, "but we lost all our money." My mother hated being poor. I told her once, "We're not so poor."

She glared at me.

"We have food and a house and—"

She stopped me cold in the middle of my sentence. "What does a boy know about money?"

I didn't argue with her. My mother didn't like people to disagree with her.

All my aunts lived in El Paso and sometimes we would stay with them on weekends. My aunts, they weren't really rich. But they weren't really poor, either. When we went to El Paso, my mother would take me shopping and buy me clothes. She told me once, "The clothes here are a better quality." She had this thing about quality. She liked elegant and beautiful things. She had lots of jewelry and she wore it all the time—rings and necklaces and earrings and bracelets. I think she probably thought my father wasn't a quality man. Or maybe he couldn't *buy* her quality—elegant, beautiful things. All he gave her was me.

I just couldn't get my mind off where my mom got the money to buy me clothes, to pay for rent, to buy food, to do anything. She had a car and she had the money to put gas in it and she had nice dresses—but she didn't work. She told me she did, but I knew she didn't.

When I was about nine, things started to get weird. My mother started to disappear more and more. I would come home from school and the house would be empty. Sometimes she would be gone for more than a week. She would give me money to buy myself food or whatever I needed. She never gave me Mexican pesos. It was always American dollars. Sometimes when I woke up in the morning, there was no one home but me. And then sometimes she would spend days and days in bed. I would make her soup. Well, I didn't actually make the soup. I just went to the store and bought it and opened the can and warmed it up. She didn't eat it anyway. I didn't know what was wrong. And I asked her, "Maybe you should go to a doctor?"

"A doctor?" she said.

"Yeah. I think maybe you're sick."

She gave me one of her looks. I didn't like those looks. It was her way of slapping me. We lived that way for about a year, her slapping me with her looks.

And after awhile, I didn't want to be around my mother anymore. It made me sad. And it made me mad too.

One day a man knocked on the door. I was reading a book and I had the radio on. I never knew whether I should open the door or not. My mom never gave me too many rules. She did tell me I shouldn't speak to strangers. But I spoke to strangers all the time and nothing bad ever happened. So I just decided to answer the door. A man stood there and he seemed nice. He was wearing a suit and he was wearing cologne and he seemed nice. "Is your mother here?" he asked. His English was perfect.

"No," I said. "She's not here."

"Do you know when she'll be back?"

"No," I said.

"Your English is good," he said.

"I speak Spanish too," I said. "I like Spanish better than English."

He laughed. He took out a big brown envelope. "Give this to your mother," he said.

I nodded.

He reached into his pocket and gave me a ten dollar bill. "This is for you," he said.

I nodded. And when my mother came home, I gave her the envelope and told her he'd given me ten dollars.

She looked at me and said, "Don't ever answer the door if I'm not here." She gave me a crooked smile. "I have to get dressed. Now, go on and play with Jorge."

She always told me that. "Go on and play with Jorge."

So that's the way it was. I spent a lot of time at Jorge's house. Not that I minded. And Jorge and his family, they didn't mind either. His mother was nice and I ate dinner there almost every night and I would teach her a little English. And my life was okay. Eating at Jorge's became normal and Jorge felt like a brother. He and Marcos didn't get along, and that wasn't so great, but they both liked me and somehow we managed to hang out together all the time. We were like a team. Since my bike had been stolen, they got together and stole another bike—and gave it to me. That made me really happy. You really have to like someone to steal a bike for them.

But when I'd come home, I was alone. I hated that. I would read books. And I would watch television. I liked the *telenovelas*. When I got tired of *telenovelas*, I would draw. I liked to draw. Sometimes I think books and *telenovelas* and drawing saved my life.

3.

It was a Thursday, I remember that. That evening, my mother came walking through the door. She was drunk. Really drunk. She kissed me and I could smell cigarettes and alcohol on her breath. She told me she was sorry, sorry for everything and that everything was going to change. Everything was going to be better. I helped her get to bed. I gave her a glass of water. In the morning when I woke up, she was still sleeping. I got ready for school. I didn't need her help with that. When I came home that Friday afternoon, my mother was making dinner. I remember that meal. She made *sopa de fideo* and *chiles rellenos*. It was the best meal I'd ever had. I studied her and I knew she was sad and there was nothing I could do to make her happy.

And then she said, "Let's spend the night in El Paso."

"Sounds great," I said.

We crossed the bridge and my mother showed the border guys her passport and then we took a taxi to my aunt's house.

I remember watching television with my cousins. I remember my mom telling me that she had to leave and that she would be back in the morning. I remember seeing a strange look on my aunt's face.

I slept on a bed with my cousin Rafie. I was afraid my mother wasn't coming back. But she *did* come back. She had a suitcase with her. The suitcase was full of all my clothes.

I looked at her and she said, "I'm going to take you to meet your father."

I didn't say anything. Maybe I did. I don't remember. I was scared. That's what I remember.

My aunt drove us to the place where my father lived, a small house that was close to downtown. When we stopped, my mother got out and knocked on the door. A man came out. He was thin and handsome and tall and had black hair. My aunt was watching me. "That's your father," she said. "You look like him."

I nodded.

I noticed that my mother and the man who was my father were arguing. I couldn't hear what they were saying. They were standing on the front porch of the red brick house. Finally, I heard my mother yelling "You sonofabitch, you have to fucking take him!"

She put the suitcase on the steps of the porch and walked away.

She opened the door to the car and looked at me. "You're going to live with your father." She sounded angry.

I didn't say anything. I wanted to ask her why all of this was happening. But I knew she wasn't going to tell me. My mother never liked to talk about anything.

I got out of the car and looked at her.

She looked back at me. "Do you hate me?"

I didn't know if I hated her or not. I just wanted to go back to Juárez. I wanted to go back to my life.

She asked me again. "Do you hate me?"

"Yes," I said. "I hate you." And then I just walked toward the man who was my father. I didn't look back, didn't wave, didn't say goodbye. If she didn't want me, then I didn't want her either.

That was the last time I saw her.

I didn't hate her.

4.

I remember my father staring at the suitcase sitting on the steps. "Your mother says you speak English."

"Yes," I said.

"That's good," he said.

We kept studying each other. I was thin like him. I had his hazel eyes, his thick brown hair, his thin lips. I even had dimples like him. "Your mother didn't tell me about you."

"She didn't tell me about you either."

"Yeah, well, your mother doesn't like to talk. I have that in common with her." He didn't seem all that happy to have me around. "I didn't plan on this." Then he mumbled something and I didn't quite understand what he'd said. He spoke with a Texas accent even though he looked Mexican. I didn't like it. He shook his head at me. "You don't talk much, do you?"

"Mom said I shouldn't talk to strangers."

That made him laugh. "So you're a fucking comedian."

I didn't think it was funny.

He took me inside the house. It was neat and spare. He had a leather chair and a leather couch and a television. There was a rug on the wood floor. There wasn't much to the kitchen. He had a stove and a refrigerator but he didn't have pots, pans, spices, stuff like that. He had a coffeemaker. I guess he didn't cook much. I didn't know how to cook either so I guess I thought I was going to have to learn.

The bathroom was really dirty. There were a couple towels on the floor and the toilet had stains and the bathroom mirror was broken. "Your job is to keep this bathroom clean," he said. "I'll get you some cleaning stuff. I'll fix that mirror. You do know how to clean, don't you?"

I nodded.

He showed me a bedroom in the back. "This is your room," he said. There was nothing in it. He looked at me. I guess I looked sad. "You can cry. But after the first week, no more crying. I don't like people who cry about things."

He had a big black pick-up truck that was sparkling clean. We drove to a huge home improvement store. I'd never been in a store that big. We bought paint. I got to pick the color. I picked white. I picked a lamp. I picked a rug for my room. He bought cleaning supplies. "I want you to keep your room clean. And the kitchen, keep that clean too."

And then we went to a furniture store. He bought me a one-person bed. He bought me a bookshelf and a desk. "You're going to study," he said. "You're going to read books, you're going to make straight A's in school. If you don't, you'll be out on the goddamned streets."

I nodded.

Then we went to another store and he bought me some blankets for my bed and some curtain rods and some curtains. We painted the room that afternoon. Mostly, he painted it. I watched, but I did the corners with a brush just like he told me to. We didn't talk. He didn't ask me questions. I didn't ask him questions either. He listened to country music. I had never listened to the radio in English and I thought that the songs were sad.

I slept on the couch that night.

I was sad and I was confused. It took me a long time to fall asleep. I listened to all the sounds on the street, an ambulance, the train, cars coming and going. I thought, at first, that my life in El Paso was going to be just like my life in Juárez—only the language would be different. I tried not to think about bad things. I tried not to think about my mother. But I did think about her and I thought about Marcos and Jorge and then I started to cry and I cried for a long time. And then I stopped.

And really, my father didn't seem to be such a bad guy. He wasn't nice like Jorge's father, but he was getting stuff for me and making sure I had my own room and I knew he was going to give me rules that I had to follow, and if I followed them, then he'd take care of me.

When I woke up in the morning, we moved the furniture in. He hung up my curtains. He told me to sweep and mop the floor.

I nodded.

"So do it then," he said. "Then make your bed."

He looked around the room and nodded. "I'm going to take a shower," he said.

I walked around the house. There was a nice big room with lots of windows that faced the backyard. It had a brick floor and I liked the room a lot but it didn't have anything in it. It was empty and that's how I felt—empty. I walked into the backyard. It was just dirt and weeds and a nice big tree.

I walked to the living room and thought about watching television but I didn't feel like it, so I walked out to the front porch and sat on the front steps. There was a newspaper in the front yard and I sat on the steps and started to read it.

I could hear the bells of the cathedral and then I heard my father's voice. "You're going to church. I'll let you skip this Sunday. But starting next Sunday, you're going to church every week. Have you made your communion?"

"No," I said.

"How old are you?"

"Ten."

"You should have made your communion," he said.

"Mom didn't go to church," I said.

"I don't go to church either," he said. "But that's no excuse." He shook his head. Then he looked at me, like he was studying me. "What's your name?"

"Maximiliano."

"They call you Max?"

"Yeah."

"What's your last name?"

"Gonzalez."

"That's your mother's name. We'll have to fix that. Your last name's McDonald."

"McDonald? You're not Mexican?"

"Yeah, I'm Mexican. Look, not every Mexican has a Mexican name." He laughed. "Maximiliano McDonald." He laughed again. "It's got a ring to it. Where were you born?"

I shrugged. "Here. El Paso. But I don't know where."

"Guess I'll have to do some paperwork. Have that name changed. Legally, I mean." He looked at his watch. "I'll be gone for the day. I have some business." He took out a twenty dollar bill. "Get yourself some food. If you walk down that way," he pointed directly ahead of us, "and you walk up Mesa Street, you'll find places." He put a key in my hand. "Don't lose it or I'll kick your ass." He started walking toward his pickup truck in the driveway. He turned back, "And don't ever walk into my room. Not ever."

When my father left, I cleaned the bathroom. That took a while. Then I took a shower. I looked through my clothes, hung them up in my closet. They were a little wrinkled. I looked everywhere but I couldn't find an iron. I'd been ironing my own clothes since I started school. Besides teaching me to read and write in English, it was the only other thing my mother had taught me how to do.

My mother had put a picture of herself in my suitcase. She was smiling and she looked like she was happy. But photographs lied. They always lied. I put the picture in my desk drawer.

I put on a T-shirt and I decided to take a walk. I walked all day in every direction. I had nowhere to go and I didn't have my aunt's phone number and didn't know how to get there on my own. I thought of walking over to Juárez but I was afraid of getting lost.

I bought a yellow pad and some pens and a drawing pad and some pencils and a pencil sharpener. I wasn't hungry and I didn't eat anything. I got home before dark and sat at my desk and wrote down all my father's rules.

1. Make straight A's at school.
2. Clean bathroom and kitchen once a week.
3. Go to church on Sundays and make my first communion.
4. Never go into his room.
5. Don't lose the key to the house.

I knew there would be more rules. And I was ready to write them down. So that was the way it was going to be with me and him, this man who was my father. He was the rule maker. I was the rule follower.

And then I sketched my room and put the sketch pad under my bed. It wasn't a very good drawing. But I didn't care.

And then, before I put my yellow writing pad away, I wrote down my new name: Maximiliano McDonald. I liked Gonzalez better.

5.

My father sent me to St. Patrick's. I could walk there from where we lived. I knew the school wasn't free. My father, who I called Eddie behind his back, said when the time came to go to high school, he was going to send me to Cathedral. I asked him what kind of school that was. "It's a Catholic boys' school."

I nodded. I did a lot of nodding around my father.

I got used to living in El Paso. I had friends. I liked school. I made A's. There was nothing special about my life. And special wasn't something I expected. I learned how to cook, sort of. I could fry eggs and I learned to make omelets because my father liked them. I knew how to make hamburgers. We ate a lot of sandwiches. We ate a lot of pizza and take-out food. My father and I would watch television together sometimes. But he went out at night a lot. I think I was numb, that's what I think. I've been numb most of my life. That's how I've survived.

When school ended that year, I hung out at the house a lot. I checked out books from the library and read and read and read.

Like my mother, my father didn't work. He spent a lot of time on the phone and a lot of time in his room and he would take off in his truck. Sometimes he didn't come home at night. I asked him about that.

"Are you my mother?" he said. But then he said, "Do you get afraid when you're alone at night?"

"No. Mom used to leave me alone all the time."

"What kind of a mother does that?"

I shrugged. "Look, alone doesn't scare me. It's just that I worry."

"Worry?"

"What if you don't come home? What will I do?"

He didn't say anything for a while, and then he said. "I like women. Do you understand what I'm saying?"

"Yeah," I said.

"So don't worry."

"Okay," I said. "I won't worry." And then I asked him, "Why don't you work?"

"I do work," he said. "I'm a businessman."

"What kind of businessman?" I asked.

"You'll find out on your own," he said. "And I don't like you hanging around the house so much."

I shrugged. *Where was I supposed to go?*

"Listen, Max, you know how to swim?"

"No," I said.

"Learn," he said.

Another rule.

"When's your birthday?" he asked.

"Next week. June seventh."

"I'll get you a bike." That made me happy. He didn't throw me a birthday party, but then my mother had never thrown me a party either. And anyway, I didn't like parties. But I liked the bike. I would ride around with Pete, a friend from school. I asked Pete if he knew how to swim and he said yes. So he taught me how to swim. It was a good summer: swimming, reading and riding my bike. It wasn't such a bad life.

One afternoon when I got home, there was a man in our living room. "Hi," I said.

He nodded at me.

I looked at him and asked, "Where's my dad?"

"He's getting something for me," he said.

I turned on the television.

My father came into the room with a package wrapped in brown paper. He handed the man the package and the man handed my father a wad of money. They went outside and talked, then the man left.

When my father came back inside, he looked at me and said, "Never talk about what I do."

I nodded.

He handed me two twenties and a ten. "I'm giving you fifty dollars a month for your allowance."

"Thanks," I said.

"If you're smart, you won't spend it all and you'll put some away."

"Okay," I nodded. I wondered if saving money was a rule. It didn't sound like a rule. It was more like a suggestion. *Never talk about what I do.* That was a rule. So I started separating suggestions from rules.

After a while, I figured it out. My father was a drug dealer. I don't think I cared, not really. And what was I supposed to do about it anyway? Some of his customers seemed really normal. Some guys came by in business suits. Some guys looked liked normal college kids. Others, not so normal. I really liked to study the guys who came to do business with my father if they had tattoos. One guy had a tattoo of a mermaid on his shaved head. I had a thing for tattoos.

One morning, I asked my father, "Can I get a tattoo?"

We were eating breakfast. I'd made him a cheese and jalapeño omelet. "No fuckin' way," he said.

"Not even if I pay for it with my allowance and the money I save?"

"I said no fuckin' way."

"So that's another rule," I said.

"You're goddamned right," he said.

I guess I must have looked sad or disappointed because he said, "Look, you're a good kid, and you're gonna stay a good kid."

"Dad, what if I'm not really good?"

He smiled. "That's the first time you've ever called me *Dad*."

"You want me to call you Eddie?"

"No, Dad works."

I nodded. "Look, Dad, maybe I'm not a good kid. It's not like you know me."

"You're soft," he said.

"I'm not." I hated him for saying that.

He could tell I was mad. He put his hand on my shoulder. He hardly ever touched me. "I know a few things. I know what I see."

I did hate him. I did.

6.

Sometimes I would take out the picture of my mother and stare at it. I took out my pencil and tried to draw her. I couldn't remember her first name. But I didn't want to forget her face.

7.

One day my father came into the room and handed me my birth certificate. I stared at it. I saw the name on the birth certificate: Maximiliano Gonzalez McDonald.

I looked at my father. "Thought I was gonna have to change your name. Turns out you had my name all along."

I nodded.

"Why'd she name you Maximiliano?"

"She thought the story of Emperor Maximiliano and the Empress Carlota was romantic."

My father laughed — then shook his head. He looked a little sad. "Carlota was mad. Fucking crazy. Just like your mother."

8.

I made my first communion when I was eleven. I was about four years older than the other kids. Not that I cared all that much. From the very beginning, I knew that I would never be a very good Catholic. I wasn't interested in God and I didn't think he was interested in me either. We sort of just ignored each other. I was going to do the Catholic thing because it was one of my father's rules. I guess he figured that the church thing would make me a better person. But this was what I didn't really get: if my dad thought that going to church made you a better person, then why didn't he go to mass? Maybe he didn't want to be a better person? But if he didn't want to be a better person, then why would he want me to be a better person? Maybe I thought too much about things.

On the Saturday before my first communion, my father bought me a new pair of black pants, a new pair of shoes, a new white shirt, my first tie and my first sports coat. He took me to mass that Sunday. It was strange. I was used to going by myself. He was all dressed up, wore a suit and shaved. He looked really handsome. Before he left the house, he handed me a rosary. It was old and worn. He just handed it to me and said, "It belonged to my father."

I took it and looked at him. He looked sad. "He came over from Ireland when he was a young man. He settled in Guanajuato. Married a woman named Rosario. I was born in San Antonio. And that about sums up what I have to say about my family history."

I wanted to ask him if he'd loved his father, but I thought he'd hate me for asking the question. I smiled at him, "This is better than an allowance." I put it my pocket.

After mass, we stood outside the cathedral and one of my friends took a picture of me and my father. My father actually smiled. Then he took me out for breakfast. A woman named Blanca met us at the restaurant. She was pretty and she had a present for me. "I'm a friend of your father's."

I shook her hand. "My name's Maximiliano," I said. "Most people call me Max."

"It's a beautiful name," she said.

"You can open your present," she said.

It was a pen. An expensive one. "Your father says you write a lot." I wondered if he read the things I wrote in my journal. I thought about making a rule that he couldn't go in my room either. I smiled at her and thanked her. She was nice and she liked to talk and to laugh. We had a really nice breakfast and I wondered if maybe my father would marry her and quit his business and we could maybe live a normal life. Deep down inside I knew it would never happen.

Blanca asked me what I wanted to do when I grew up. I could tell my father was interested in my answer. "Well, I'd either like to be a musician or an artist."

She smiled at me. "Do you play an instrument?"

"No."

"Do you draw?"

"Yes," I said.

My father was surprised. "What do you draw?" she asked.

"The tree in the backyard. My room. My desk. My dad's truck." I didn't tell her about drawing my mother over and over again.

"You've been drawing my truck?"

"Yes," I said.

He never asked to see that drawing. But a year later, when I was better at drawing, I gave him a charcoal sketch of his truck for Christmas. I framed it and everything.

"It's good," he said. He had a strange look on his face. I thought for a moment that he was going to cry, but my father wasn't a crier—and the look went away. Just like Blanca had gone away.

9.

I was a quiet and serious boy. I was even more serious and quiet when I entered high school. I made friends, but they were school friends. I didn't want anyone coming over to my house. My dad had too many customers coming in and out at all hours of the day and night. And I guess I had a theory as to why my father had bought a house in this neighborhood. The house next door had burned down and no one had bothered to raze it to the ground. The rest of the houses were rentals and the houses weren't kept up and half the renters around us all seemed like they were potential customers for my father's business. It was all perfect.

Our front yard wasn't kept up and my father wanted to keep it that way. "I like weeds," he said. "Nothing wrong with weeds. You want a nice lawn in this neighborhood? What's wrong with you? You want people to notice us?"

I hated weeds. I guess you could say I always liked everything nice and neat—even though I knew that everything was chaos. I decided to make a deal with my father. I fixed the backyard. I planted some bushes and I grew a nice lawn. It wasn't a big yard. It had a big fence around it and no one could look in. I think my dad liked the backyard. He bought some lawn chairs and sometimes we would both sit out in the evening. I would read a book and he would read the newspaper. My dad had a thing for reading newspapers.

About the same time I entered Cathedral High School, my father began using some of the products he sold. He began to smoke marijuana in his room. I could smell it. A lot of the times he would come out of his room and I could tell he was stoned because he whistled. He always whistled when he was stoned.

One Friday night, I was thinking about meeting some of my school friends at a football game. I was reading a book and eating a sandwich in the kitchen. My father walked in and grabbed a beer from the refrigerator. He sort of smiled at me and patted me on the back. I liked when he did that, but that only happened about twice a year and I would have liked it better if he hadn't been stoned. "What are you reading?"

"A story by Hemingway," I said.

"Famous guy," he said. And then he just nodded. "You know, you can drink if you want. Drinking is okay. Just don't overdo it. And don't ever drive when you're drunk."

"Okay," I said. "But you don't have to worry about me drinking and driving, Dad. I don't drive."

"Aren't you old enough?"

"I'll be sixteen."

"June seventh."

I was glad he remembered my birthday—even though he didn't remember how old I was.

"You can get a permit."

"Guess so."

"I know a guy who teaches people how to drive. He has a little business."

"Is he one of your customers?"

My father didn't answer the question. I could tell he didn't like that I'd asked. I shrugged. "Sorry."

My father nodded, downed his beer and said, "Just remember that you can drink." It almost sounded like another rule. It sounded like I was supposed to start.

He didn't come back for a few days, but by then he'd gotten me a cell phone so I could call or text him if I got too worried. He said people who were worriers never changed. "You can't help it," he said. He made it sound like worrying was a sickness.

That Sunday night, I texted him. *U ok?* A few minutes later, he texted me back. *I like wmen. Do ur hmwork.* I like women, I like women, I like women. Bullshit, I thought. It's not just women. It's women who like to party. By then, I knew from being around my dad's customers that partying meant drugs plus sex. I knew what he was up to. I tried not to let it upset me, *but it did upset me.* But what the fuck was I supposed to do about it anyway? I would never rat him out and I would never run away from home. Those were things I just didn't have in me. I wondered if that made me a good boy or a bad boy. Maybe I was just an afraid boy.

10.

A couple of guys came over one evening. I knew what was happening. My father went into his room. The two guys were smoking cigarettes on the porch and I could hear what they were saying. "This connect has good shit."

So that's what my father was—a connect.

After a few months, I realized my father had what other businessmen would call a diversified portfolio. He dealt in marijuana, cocaine, crack, ecstasy, heroin and crystal meth. I looked up all the drugs on the Internet. I knew all about them.

My father came into my room one night. All he said was, "If you ever do drugs, I'll beat the holy shit out of you and kick your ass out on the street."

When he left my room, I sort of laughed. He was like fucking Moses writing down the Ten Commandments.

I put the new rule at the top of the list.

11.

My father got a credit card in my name. My allowance increased from fifty dollars a month to a hundred dollars a month—but I was supposed to make the payments on my own credit card. He opened a bank account for me. "How much money have you saved?" he asked me.

"About four hundred dollars," I said.

He nodded. "Good."

"You have to learn how to handle your finances." Another rule.

These are the things my father bought me that year:

1. Driving lessons.
2. An Apple computer.
3. An iPhone.
4. A brand new Volkswagen.

It's not as if I didn't know where the money came from. I did wonder how he laundered his money. But I found some lawyer's name on a business card on the coffee table one day. I didn't know many things about my father. I knew he didn't like to talk. And I also knew that he was a very smart man. *I guess he was a real businessman.*

12.

I had a habit of riding the bus on weekends. I would get on a bus and ride around and think. One Saturday, two women—I guessed they made a living by cleaning houses—were having a conversation. I liked listening to their Spanish and it reminded me of Juárez and of my boyhood. Everything had become so much more complicated since then. I just kept listening to them. One of the women was telling the other woman that the streets of Juárez were becoming rivers of blood. She spoke about a young woman the soldiers took away who was never seen again, and they spoke of the kidnappings and beheadings and houses where people were found tortured. They talked about all the women who had disappeared.

I drifted away from their conversation, wondering what it would be like to take a gun to someone's head, to kidnap someone, to torture a man. What would it be like to cut someone's hands off? I knew there was a listserve that counted the bodies because I had joined that listserve. It was all about the dead bodies. The thing was that the bodies didn't have names. Sometimes I made up names for them.

I had a whole list of names.

This whole thing, I thought, this whole thing was because of men like my father.

I went out with some friends that night. I got drunk and I woke up the next day and discovered I was at Pete's house. I had never felt that bad.

Pete walked into the living room and laughed. "You really let loose last night."

Oh shit, I thought. Had I said something about my father? "I don't remember. What did I do? What did I say?"

"You kissed Sandra."

"What?"

"No worries, dude, she kissed you back."

"Really?" That sort of made me a little bit happy.

"Yeah, you sort of made out all night."

"That's nice," I said.

"You were really drunk. But what have you got against 420?"

"Why?"

"Dave offered you a joint and I thought you were going to cut his fucking head off. We had to pull you away and cool you off."

I shrugged. "I just don't do drugs," I said.

"420's cool."

"I don't do weed. I don't do drugs. End of story."

"Straight-edger, huh?

"Pretty much."

"Well, that's cool too." Pete laughed. "But you really did let loose on that liquor, dude."

I looked at my phone. I had a text from my father. *U ok?* That made me happy, that he was wondering where I was. I smiled and texted him back: *I like women* ☺.

It was the first time I had successfully joked around with my father. I knew it was a joke that would make him smile.

As I drove home that afternoon, I decided to get a passport. I don't remember what had happened to the one I had. My mother had always kept it in her possession. I wanted to go to Juárez. I wanted to find Marcos and Jorge. I wanted to see what they had become. Or maybe I wanted to find out what I had become.

13.

It took me three months to get my passport. When I got it in the mail, it also included my border crossing card. My father intercepted my mail. I didn't like that—but I never crossed my father. I was afraid of him. I'd seen his temper, and though his temper had never been aimed at me, I knew what could happen. Maybe that's why I kept all his rules.

He asked me why I wanted a passport.

"To go to Juárez to visit my old friends."

"Don't you think it's been too long? Don't you think they've moved on?"

"I don't know," I said. And I was really mad—and though I never talked back to my father—this time I did. "And you don't know either."

"No fuckin' way you're going to Juárez. Don't you read the goddamned newspapers? Don't you fuckin' know what's happening over there?"

"I know."

"For such a smart kid, you're something of a dumbass."

I nodded, and took my passport out of his hand. "I have a rule," I said. "Never open my mail. And never walk into my room."

I didn't bother to study the look on his face. I grabbed my passport out of his hand and turned away from him.

14.

I think I knew something about addiction. I was addicted to drawing my mother. I had hundreds of sketches of her.

I never sketched my father.

15.

I heard my father talking to a man. He was in the kitchen and I was doing my homework on my laptop while I watched television. My father was excited and I noticed his cell phone was on the coffee table. I knew he was using one of those throwaway cells. Once when we were on our way to eat dinner, we took the scenic route. He stopped to toss a cell phone out into the desert. My father was saying something about his fuckin' ship coming in.

He left on a business trip. "I'll be back in a couple of weeks," he said. "I won't be in touch." He gave me the business card I'd seen, the one with the lawyer's name and number and address. "If something happens, call him."

I nodded.

He must have left early in the morning, because when I got up the next day, he was gone. He left me a note on the kitchen table. *Don't go to Juárez.*

Don't go into my room. Don't fuckin' do drugs. And start thinking about what college you want to go to. That's your homework. So every night I would come home from school, do my homework, then get on the Internet and study all the schools I might like to go to. I stayed up until two or three in the morning every night. I got lost in the homework my father gave me. It helped to keep me from worrying. In the end, I made the following list:

1. Georgetown
2. University of Texas
3. University of Chicago
4. Stanford
5. UCLA
6. Brown
7. Washington University
8. Berkeley
9. Northwestern
10. Harvard

I didn't want to go to Harvard, but if it hadn't been on the list, it would have made my father mad. So I made another list and put Harvard as number one—even though in my world it was number ten. I don't know what I had against Harvard. And anyway, it was just an assignment for my father. I doubted any of these schools would take me.

My father came home from his business trip on the last day of school of my junior year. I was happy to see him. That was the first time my father ever hugged me. And it was the first time that he seemed really happy. "Everything's going to be just fine," he said.

He was smiling and he looked so young to me and I thought that maybe now he would quit the business. He had money now. Real money, so maybe he would quit. But I was just fantasizing. Something inside me knew that this is what he knew. This is what he loved. I loved reading and drawing and music and writing. And my father, well, he loved his business. Everyone had to love something.

"Maybe," he said, "we should think about getting you an apartment. You know, so you could live on your own. So you could get used to it. You know, like a practice run before you go away to college."

"I don't need to practice," I said.

"I hear that tone," he said. "You don't get mad much—but when you get mad, you really get pissed off."

"I must get that from someone," I said. "Look, Dad, I follow your rules. I follow every fucking rule—and so now you're throwing me out?"

"It's not like that. Look, there's a lot of shit that goes down here. I don't want you in the middle of it."

"I *am* in the middle of it, Dad."

I sat down and put my face in my hands. I took a breath. And then another. I walked into my room and took out my list. I walked back into the living room and handed my list to my father. "I did my homework." I handed him the list. "And how am I going to get the money to go to any of these schools, Dad?"

"Don't worry about the money."

"Like I said, Dad, *I am in the middle of all this*. I'm in the middle of all the shit that goes down in this house. And I'm not moving. Not unless you're fucking throwing me out."

"Watch your mouth."

"Is that another rule?"

He was quiet. He bit the side of his mouth. He was in too good a mood to fight me. He studied my list. "Harvard," he whispered. "Get dressed. Let's go to a nice place."

My father wanted to know my reasoning for picking the schools I put on my list. So I did all the talking at dinner. He asked questions. I answered them. It was the longest conversation we'd ever had. I guess it was because we didn't have to talk about ourselves. He was going to put some money into my education and he wanted to know what he was getting himself into. He was an investor. It was more like a business transaction than a conversation.

16.

Harvard said no. My dad was pissed. "Fuck Harvard," he said. My sentiments exactly. The day I got an acceptance letter from Georgetown, my father was out. His addictions were getting worse and I couldn't talk to him about it. I told him I was worried. He said, "People who worry never change." I wanted to tell him that addicts never change either. But I said nothing.

I left my father a note: GOT INTO GEORGETOWN! I went out with my friends to celebrate. I had fun. I was happy. I was so, so happy. When I walked into the living room that night, the house was full of people. Some guy was snorting coke. My father must have been in the kitchen or in his room. I recognized some of his guests. I suppose some of them were more than just clients.

Some guy came up to me. He smiled. He sort of scared me, but I relaxed. Hell, I was really drunk. The guy offered me a glass pipe. It was just a little straight glass tube. I'd seen them before. I knew what those little glass tubes were used for. "You ever smoke?"

I shook my head.

"Try it," he said.

And I wanted to—I wanted to try it, to see what it was like. To know, to really know what it was all about.

He handed me the pipe.

I took it.

He reached into his pocket and unfolded a piece of tin foil. He took out a little piece of white rock. "You're gonna like this, kid," he said. And then I saw my father standing next to him. It all happened so fast. "Motherfucker!" My father's face was grotesque and contorted. He was pounding the shit out of him, pounding and pounding—and when the guy was on the floor, my father was kicking him and kicking him and I thought, for a moment, that my father was going to kill this man. Some of my father's friends were yelling for him to stop but he wouldn't stop, couldn't stop, and finally some men had to pull him away.

My father stared down at the man, just stared down at him. "Get that motherfucker out of here."

The man that had offered me the pipe was all bloody—but he was alive and moaning. A few guys dragged him out of the house.

My father looked at me said, "Give me that pipe."

I handed it to him.

"I'll kill you if you ever come near one of those pipes again. *I will fucking kill you.*"

I nodded. I was so ashamed. I walked into my room. I'd never felt so empty in all of my life.

17.

My father never mentioned what happened that night. I always wondered if he thought about it. I always thought about it.

18.

My father and I flew to Washington in July. It was hard for him to do without his drugs, so he drank a lot and I suppose that helped. We were there for a week. At night, he would disappear. I knew he'd found what he was looking for. During the day, we took in the sights, father and son. My father knew a man who'd died in Vietnam and we looked for his name on the wall—and we found it. My father traced his finger on the letters that formed the name of his friend. He didn't tell me about the man, didn't say a word about him.

My father seemed so normal that day.

We found an apartment for me. I knew it was expensive. But my father sent me away when he made the arrangements.

On the plane ride back to El Paso, I asked my father, "Are you sure you can afford that apartment, Dad?"

"Remember that trip when my ship came in?"

"Yes," I said.

That's when the conversation ended.

19.

I was sitting in the backyard, pad in hand. I was making a list of the things I needed to take with me when I drove to Washington. Me and my lists. I was drinking a beer and I was trying to imagine what my life was going to look like as a student at Georgetown University. I wondered if I would miss my father. And it was odd, but the thought occurred to me that I had stopped missing my mother. It was as if she had never existed and there was a blank piece in my heart that would live there permanently. Not a wound, not a hurt, but a blank piece.

My father stumbled into the backyard. He looked like shit and I could tell he was coming down from his last high. He sat down on the lawn chair next to mine. He lit a cigarette and his hands were shaking. "Can you bring me a beer?"

I walked into the kitchen, grabbed a beer, walked back into the backyard and handed it to him.

"Dad, you have to stop."

He just looked at me. "Who the fuck do you think you are?"

"You have to stop, Dad."

I was standing above him. He took a drink from his beer. He got up, looked me straight in the eye. "Say it again. Go on, say it again."

I looked right back at him. I never took my eyes off him. "You have to stop."

And then I felt his fist on my jaw and I fell back on the ground. I took a breath and closed my eyes. I just lay for a while, feeling the pain in my jaw. My lip was bleeding. My father looked down at me. "Get up," he said.

I got up slowly. Then I heard his voice. "You haven't earned the right to tell your father what to do."

I nodded. I wanted to hide my tears from him but I wasn't strong enough. I sat there and cried, tears falling from my face. I wanted to howl, but I kept the howl inside me. I don't know how long I sat there. I heard my father's voice. "Here," he said as he handed me a beer. "Have a beer with your old man."

20.

After a week, there wasn't much of a sign of my father's fist on my jaw or my lip. I would not wear the scar of that afternoon on my face. That's not where I would keep it.

21.

The day before I left for Georgetown, my father bought me a new car. It was practical, a Prius, not my father's style, but the kind of car he imagined his son should have. I thanked him. I think we even hugged. Yes, I hugged him. And he hugged me back. He was on something, I knew. By then, he was almost always on something. We went to dinner and he was shaking. He ordered a nice bottle of red wine and we drank together and I wanted to cry, but I didn't.

I don't remember what we talked about, but my father wasn't in any hurry that night to get anywhere. He wanted to be with me that last night. And I wanted to be with him.

After dinner, he looked at me, smiled and said, "Let's go get our passports."

I didn't know what he meant.

"Let's go have a drink at the Kentucky Club."

"In Juárez?"

"Yeah."

"But, you said—"

"It's where you were raised. Don't you want to have a drink with your old man where it all started?"

"Where it all started?"

"It's where your mother and I used to go."

He smiled. I'll always remember that smile.

22.

The only thing I remember about having a drink with my father at the Kentucky Club was my father telling me that he'd loved my mother. "I loved her." And then I knew. She was the one. She hadn't loved him back.

23.

The morning I left the house where I became a man, my father helped me put my things in the car. I didn't have much. My father was wordless. And I was too. "Bye, Dad," I said.

"Bye, son," he said.

He looked sad. He just stood there as I drove away.

24.

I'm sitting here in my Georgetown apartment and I'm thinking about my dad.

I'm packing a few things and I'm going back home. He's on a respirator. He overdosed. Heroin, meth, I don't know. It all seems so predictable, so inevitable. His attorney called me. "You need to come home and see to your dad," he said. I'm going back to take him off the respirator. I know that's what he would have wanted. At last, I can give him something. Something that matters.

I just finished reading the journal I kept when I lived with him, my father. Every rule he ever made me follow is in my journal. I can almost hear his voice. I'm holding the rosary he gave me for my first communion, the one that belonged to his father. I'm staring at the picture of us in front of the cathedral, taken at my first communion.

I always told myself I didn't know my father. I sometimes told myself that I hated him. I always told myself that he didn't know me. But that wasn't true. It wasn't true at all. I knew him. I really knew him. My girlfriend Emma, she asked me what kind of man my father was. "Who was he, Max?" she asked. "You never talk about him."

"No, I never do."

She wiped the tears from my face.

"He punched me out once," I said. And then I laughed. "My father," I whispered. "His name was Eddie. Not Edward, but *Eddie*. He was the man who saved my life. That's who he was."

BROTHER IN ANOTHER LANGUAGE

I.

Instead of winding up dead, I wound up in a therapist's office. The therapist's name was David, a blue-eyed man, beautiful, in his forties, a hint of some of his own wounds in the way he spoke, in the way he looked out at the punishing world. He possessed a kind voice, not too soft and not overly masculine, and he had a pair of incredible hands that reminded me of the figures in a Michelangelo fresco.

I liked looking into his nearly flawless face.

I'm not the kind of guy who falls in love—but those first few months after my failed attempt at suicide, I fell in love with just about anybody who offered me anything that resembled empathy. I remember looking into the face of the nurse at the hospital and begging her to make love to me.

Her response was kind but firm, "I don't make love to my patients. And I don't make love to boys."

I was desperate and prideless. "Make me feel alive."

She stared into my pleading eyes and smiled. "Silly boy, you are alive." She combed my hair with her fingers in a way my mother never had.

When she left the room, I could still feel her fingers in my hair.

I was in the psych ward for five days. Since my parents were too devastated to come and visit me, my aunt volunteered to be their emissary. "Do you have any idea what you've done to them?" She handed me a card with a therapist's name on it and told me to be a good boy. She spoke to me in the same tone of voice that she used when she talked to her dog. In her defense, she loved her dog.

No one was more surprised than me when I found myself sitting across from David. The whole scene hangs like a still life in the back of my mind, forever in the present tense. David is sitting in a comfortable leather chair. I am sitting stiffly on a couch that is threatening to chew me up and spit me out. He is offering me a bottle of water. I shake my head no. My eyes search the room for an ashtray. David looks at the bandages on my wrists and smiles softly, "I'd have gone for a tattoo instead."

I try not to smile. I want to joke back. But there is no joke inside me and I don't say anything at all.

He is utterly comfortable in his own skin and there isn't anything formal in the way he presents himself. "What would you like to talk about, Charlie?"

"Birds."

"What is it about birds that you like?"

"They make sure their young can fly before they throw them out of the nest."

He nods. I study his face and wonder where he learned to wear empathy as comfortably as my father wore his ties. "I take it you don't like your parents."

"It's mutual."

"Well, they're paying for these sessions."

"My mother's paying for these sessions."

"Does your mother work?"

"No. She's above all that."

"Then it's your father's money."

"She has plenty of her own." I am tapping my finger on my bottom lip. "Paying for these sessions? They have serious money. It's like handing a panhandler a nickel."

I see David nodding. "But it might mean they love you."

"It might."

He studies my face. "But you have other ideas about that."

"I think paying for a therapist after—" I pause, displaying my wrists. "How would it look to let their son go without a therapist when he slits his wrists in their bedroom?"

"Their bedroom?" He doesn't nod but his face says something—though I'm not sure what. "That's an interesting choice."

"I must have thought so at the time."

"Must have?"

"I don't really remember."

"Any idea why you chose that particular site?"

"Is this the part where I get to really talk?"

"Something like that."

"We were never allowed in their bedroom—not even when we were small."

"We?"

"I had a brother."

"Had?"

"We lost him."

"Did he die?"

"No. We just lost him."

"Just lost him?"

"My mom and dad are careless people. They misplaced him."

He looks at me, wants me to say more.

So this is what I say: "He left. He never came back."

I see that he is mentally placing a note in a file in his brain labeled Charlie. That much I can tell. "Do you want to talk about your brother?"

"No."

"Do you want to talk about your parents?"

"Yeah, sure, that's who I want to talk about."

He smiles at my sarcasm.

"I think your parents are trying to help you."

"Sure they are. They're going to pay for my sessions so they can pretend they're teaching me how to fly." I offer him a smirk. "You know, like the birds."

"Yes. The birds. We're back to that."

"I told you that's what I wanted to talk about."

"Let's talk about the nest you came from."

"I hate my father." The words come out without rage and without regret. It's not difficult for me to tell David how I feel about my father.

David is studying my face. He repeats my words. "You hate your father." It almost seems like he is staring at the letters that make up that word, examining the *h*, the *a*, the *t* and then the *e*. He is trying to understand what it means to hate your own father. "Is that really true, Charlie?"

"Yes, that's really true."

"You've thought about this?"

"I'm not sure that thinking is the right word."

"Charlie? You're sure?"

"Do I sound unsure?"

He looks at me with that puzzled look. I understand he wants me to explain. No longer wanting to have this particular conversation, I just look back at him. I want to get back to the subject of birds. Or Icarus, how he flew too close to the sun.

He looks right at me and says, "Hating your father is a lot of work."

"Not really. He's made it easy."

"Is there any part of you that loves him?"

"No."

"A lot of people think they hate their fathers."

"When in fact we really love them? I think you should meet my father." I took out my wallet and handed him his card.

He is gracious enough to take it even though I am behaving like a stupid, rebellious boy. I'm sure he is making a mental note of that too.

He stares at the card. "So you tried love?"

"He doesn't know what to do with love."

"Do *you* know what to do with love, Charlie?"

"Probably not."

He smiles at me. "What about your mother?"

"What about her?"

"Does your mother—does she know what to do with love?"

"She's the same. The same but different."

"Different?"

"My father controls by words and actions. My mother controls by withholding. They arrive at the same place."

"Do you think they love each other?"

"I'm not about to walk into that desert."

"Desert?"

"You can die of thirst in a desert. You know, like all those Mexicans. They're trying to get somewhere and they'll never get there alive."

He has an interesting look on his face. "There are birds in the desert too, you know."

I laugh at his joke, then get mad at myself for laughing. I don't want to let him see that I get mad at myself so I keep talking. "I don't know anything about what exists between my father and my mother. Anything I say is a lie or a theory. If my mother had a business card, I'd hand you one of hers too."

He smiles. A smiler. The thing about smilers is that they're sincere. "So you just decided to hate him instead."

"Yeah, one day I just decided. Sure."

"I'm just trying to—"

"I know," I say. I want a cigarette. "For the record, I don't love my mother either. I just don't hate her. I feel sorry for her." I stare at my fingernails but decide against chewing on them. I smoke. I bite my nails. I chew on my knuckles. Yeah. He is waiting for an answer. "My father doesn't deserve to be loved."

"Don't you think everyone deserves to be loved?"

"You mean like even Hitler had Eva Braun?" He doesn't laugh at my joke. I tap my bottom lip with my finger again. "No," I say. "Not everyone deserves to be loved."

"What about you? Does Charlie deserve to be loved?"

"I have no fucking idea. And anyway, that's not the way it works. People get killed who don't deserve to be killed. Some people have more success than they deserve. I know about a holy man who got crucified. You get where I'm going here?"

"Yes, I get you. But we're talking about love. We're talking about you."

"The guy who got crucified doesn't count?"

"I want to talk about Charlie."

"I thought you wanted to talk about *what I wanted to talk about.*"

He nods. I think he would make a very good poker player. He's hard to read—except that I already decide that he's a good man and he is incapable of hiding his kindness.

"My father's insane," I say. I really want to say that.

"Insane?"

"Emotionally insane."

"That's an interesting way to put it."

"What else would you call someone who behaves like that? He threw my brother out of the house."

"Why?"

"I don't know. He never allowed us to mention his name again. He took all of his pictures and tossed them in the trash. He went through all of my mother's albums. He even burned his birth certificate. *Even my pictures.* He walked into my room and searched it thoroughly in front of me. He took every picture of me and my brother and ripped them to shreds in front of me. I was ten. *Yes, I think my father is insane.*"

"Well, maybe there are more appropriate ways of looking at your father's—"

I didn't let him finish his sentence. "I loved my brother. And he's gone. He's lost. He might be dead. He might be alive. I don't know. But he's gone."

"And your father took him away from you."

"You're getting the picture."

"Have you ever gone to look for your brother?"

"Where would I look?"

"Why do you think your father threw your brother out of the house?"

"I don't know."

"You must have made something up about why."

"My brother was eighteen years old. He was rebellious. He was alive. He liked to laugh. He reminded them that they were dead."

"Them? Your mother and father?"

"Who else? They've never mentioned his name. Once, I asked about him. We were just finishing dinner and I said, 'I miss Antonio.' I said, 'Is he ever coming back?' My father slapped me so hard I went flying across the room. You know what my mother did? She stared at me. And then she walked out of the room." I was trying not to chew on my knuckles. "When I was small, I used to go to my brother's room when I had bad dreams and he would hold me."

"So he was like a father?"

"No. He was like someone who loved me."

I am remembering almost every detail of my first conversation with David as I stand in front of my father's coffin at the cemetery. The priest's final prayers of commendation provide the soundtrack as I play the scene over in my head.

2.

My father was killed in a car accident. He ran a red light—and took the other driver with him. A strange and ironic ending for such a careful and controlling man. Careful in the way he dressed. Careful in the way he spoke. Careful in the way he handled his personal finances. But careless in matters of the heart. He never succeeded in controlling his own cruelty. That was his drug of choice. That was his great addiction. When he saw an opportunity to be cruel, he had to take it. He tried to cover it over with a veneer of grace and civility and that thing which he called "breeding." But he didn't quite carry it off.

The funeral mass at the cathedral was formal and disciplined. Which meant that no one shed a tear. I was half hoping that at least my mother would cry. I would have thought better of her if she had. After the final service at the cemetery, my mother had people over to the house where I was raised, the house where I had been something of an unwelcome visitor for the formative years of my life.

I don't know why people like my parents have children. My father never held me as a boy. My mother's touches were tentative.

There was no laughter in my house. Only my brother had known how to laugh.

After my suicide attempt, my father never spoke to me again. My mother, whose emotional disposition can best be described as austere, pretended it had been a mistake. That's exactly how she put it. "You made a terrible mistake, Charlie." Oddly, that was the kindest thing she'd every said to me. I think a part of my father was almost disappointed that I hadn't succeeded. He could not have possibly been as disappointed as I was.

As I tried to adjust to having survived my suicide, I took a job as a bartender.

I promised David that I would not try to off myself again.

I found a place to live in Sunset Heights. My mother said that it was a predictable choice. She looked at me in that disdainful way she'd cultivated over the years. "Just the kind of neighborhood you'd choose. And will you be living next door to a prostitute?"

"I hope so," I said.

"Just make sure she's really a woman before you sleep with her."

That made me laugh. There were moments I thought my mother had potential.

My apartment was a dump. It was an old building with worn wood floors and high ceilings. I painted the walls white, re-sanded the floors and managed to get rid of the mice. I thought it was a good sign that I'd never seen a cockroach. I started going to school part-time and decided to major in art. I had my drawings and paintings all over the apartment. Not that I was all that impressed with my own work—but it was the only art I could afford. I didn't waste a lot of time worrying about my own talent.

I had a few sketches of some girls I'd slept with. I liked studying them. Not that I went out with many girls—a few—and they always liked me more than I liked them. I don't think I could bring myself to respect someone who actually liked me. But there was one girl—her name was Ileana. She was graceful and elegant and easy to be with. She was from Juárez and spoke perfect English. She was rich and articulate in two languages. She'd studied at a boarding school in England. And she was beautiful. I always thought she was sleeping with me to get back at her parents.

She left me. Of course she did. She said she couldn't stand being around me anymore.

I asked her if she hated me.

"Oh, Charlie," she said. "Sweet, sweet, Charlie. It's so unnecessary to hate a man who hates himself as much as you do. I just can't be around to watch you anymore." And then she did something I didn't expect. She cried.

I knew there was nothing I could say to make her stay. No one had ever taught me how to love. And perhaps, in that department, I was uneducable.

I missed Ileana at first, but I had always been more in love with being alone than being in the presence of other people—even beautiful and intelligent women. I thought of her as I looked around at all the people at my father's funeral. I don't know why I expected to see her there. I kept searching all the faces. It dawned on me that the only people who were in attendance were relatives and the men and women who worked for my father in his bank. Imagine owning a bank. Imagine owning several. They had praise for my father, those people. One of the men, Mr. Gonzalez, who served as a pallbearer, told me my father was a fine and ethical man who would be deeply missed. I wanted to ask him who my father was. But the question was insipid and banal. If my father had wanted me to know who he was, he'd have let me know.

It occurred to me that my father's life had meant nothing—not even to him. Maybe there's tragedy in that—though I doubt it. Tragedy has a profound emotional quality. Certainly my father's life lacked that. He was one of millions of men who lived, made lots of money, and died. He lived his life with certainty, which meant he didn't give a damn about people like me—or most of the occupants of the earth for that matter.

My father's two brothers were there. And my mother's three sisters. I was surprised that most of my cousins were also present. They couldn't have had more than a few ounces of affection for an uncle who was by turns emotionally aloof, intellectually superior, and obscenely rich.

My cousins—every one of them—were impeccably dressed, self-possessed, good-looking people who knew how to behave themselves in public. They were in love with their own class and their own sense of entitlement. Not that I knew anything about them. And not that I felt anything when I found myself staring into their lovely faces. They had fine features, that was true enough. So did I for that matter. And what of it? It's always been interesting to me how we mistake good genes for virtue.

Marta, my cousin who was not much older than me, attempted to have a conversation. "I'm sorry about your dad."

She was being nice and I should have at least returned the favor. But of course I didn't. "He was a prick," I said.

She didn't seem surprised by what I said.

"Still, he was your father."

"Yes," I said. "He was my father." I looked at her. She was very beautiful. And I wondered if there was anything that mattered underneath all the beauty. "Do you love your father?"

She smiled. "Of course I do."

"Is he kind to you?"

"Kindness has nothing to do with love," she said.

Then it was my turn to smile.

I stayed at the reception until the end. Sometimes I had good manners too. Only my mother's sisters remained after all the guests had left. I tried to be civil. I kissed them all on the cheek as I saw myself out. One of my aunts followed me out to my car. "You'll leave your mother alone?"

"Yes," I said.

"You've always disappointed her."

"I wonder which one of us is more disappointed."

I could see she wanted to slap me. I could see her trying to control herself. I looked into my aunt's hazel eyes. "Tell my mother I never want to see her again."

"Be a man and tell her yourself."

I grabbed my aunt's arm and dragged her back into the house. I let her go when I was standing in front of my mother who was sipping on a glass of scotch.

I looked at my aunt. Then looked at my mother. "I never want to see you again." I took the drink out of her hand and downed it. "And that's the last thing I'll ever take from you."

I worked that night. The bar was busy. I made nearly two hundred dollars in tips. The money I made was all mine.

3.

The next afternoon, I was in David's comfortable office. "When they were lowering my father into the ground, I was thinking of the first time I came to your office."

David didn't say anything. He wanted me to keep talking. I didn't know what to say next so I didn't say anything at all. We sat there for a long time. He wasn't going to give in this time. He was going to make me talk.

"They sent me to the best schools," I said. "I behaved for a long time. I was the best student. I had the best grades."

"What was your favorite subject?"

"English and history."

"English and history? That's interesting."

"I loved reading books."

"You have a favorite author?"

"Dickens."

David smiled. "Hmm. Why Dickens?"

"He didn't like rich people."

David nodded. "I always thought he had a romantic view of the poor."

"Yes," I said. "I liked that about him."

David smiled. "So you liked books. Tell me about your friends about school."

"I didn't have any friends."

"None?"

"None."

"Why is that, Charlie?"

"I didn't want any."

"Why?"

"I never knew what to say."

"Really? You seem comfortable enough with words."

"I have a formal and aesthetic relationship to words."

David was smiling. Absolutely, he was a smiler. I wanted to tell him that he was very beautiful—but I didn't.

He looked at me. "What are you thinking?"

I just shrugged.

"Tell me, Charlie, why were you thinking of me at your father's funeral?"

I looked at him and told myself I wasn't going to cry. But that's exactly what was happening. There was something caught in my throat and I couldn't talk and I knew my lips were trembling. And there I was sobbing. But it was worse than that because I wasn't just sobbing, I was howling. I kept hitting my own chest as if I was trying to tell my heart not to do what it was doing, to stop hurting me, my heart, and I found myself kneeling on the floor and howling and I didn't even know why and I could hear the moaning in the room and I knew it was me who was moaning and I couldn't stop and I hated myself more than I had ever hated myself.

I don't know how long I was there on the floor, sobbing and moaning and howling. But then I felt David's hand pulling me up.

"Charlie?"

I found myself staring into his eyes as we stood there.

"I'm sorry," I said. I sat there for a while until I felt calmer. "David," I whispered, "maybe I was thinking of you because I love you. And I never loved him. I didn't love my father and *I love you*. Not him."

David seemed so calm. "And do you hate yourself for loving me and not him?"

"I'm not supposed to love you. I'm supposed to love my father."

"You don't have to love him, Charlie."

I sat down on the couch and took a breath. I hid my face. I just sat there.

"Look at me, Charlie."

He was sitting in his chair.

He was smiling at me.

I wanted to talk. But I didn't know what to say. I shrugged and looked into his kind face. "It's so sad, isn't it, David? Not to love your father. And to love a man who isn't your father, a man who gets paid to listen to you. It's so sad."

"I know it's sad, Charlie."

"I don't know what to do." I kept staring at the floor.

"Look at me," he said.

So I looked at him.

"Do you know what transference is?"

"Yes," I said. "I know what that is."

I couldn't stop the tears. I looked away. I couldn't stand his eyes. I had never known what to do in the face of kindness.

He just looked at me and I knew what he was thinking.

"There's no one in the world left to love me," I said.

"Never believe that, Charlie," he said.

"It's true."

"Charlie, do you know what countertransference is?"

"Yes," I said.

"What you feel for me is transference. What I feel for you is countertransference. We can work with that, don't you think?"

4.

A month after my father died, I got a phone call on my cell from David. "Your mother called me today, Charlie."

"If it's about your fees, I can pay."

"No, no, no," he said. "That's not what this is about."

"But I'm going to start paying for my own sessions. I just want you to know."

"Yes," he said, "we can talk about that when you come in on Tuesday. Is that okay?"

"Yes, that's good."

"Charlie, your mother said that you need to get in touch with your father's attorney. She gave me his number."

I took the number down. Before he hung up the phone, David wanted to know why I didn't ask how my mother was doing.

"I already know how she's doing," I said.

"Really?"

"Sure," I said. "She's the same."

"How do you know that?"

"Did she ask about me?"

"No. I guess she didn't."

"Like I said—she's the same."

When I hung up the phone, I sat on my bed and looked at the painting I was working on. It wasn't any good. I didn't care about the painting. I didn't know what it was, didn't know what it meant, didn't know why I was doing it.

Everything always stayed the same, the way I lived, the way I felt. I was wasting my time going to see David. Maybe I'd stop.

I took out some gesso and painted over the canvas I was working on. A fresh start. Yeah. Maybe there was a painting inside me.

I found myself in the law office of Richard Fry at 6:15 sharp. The receptionist ushered me into his office. It was exactly what I expected: an expensive and extensive law library, original art on the walls. All the accoutrements of success. He was an impossibly handsome man in his late forties, impeccably dressed, had a warm handshake and the straightest teeth I'd ever seen. The kind of man who seduced people just by walking into the room.

"Sit down," he said.

I wanted a cigarette. I had never been good at hiding the fact that I was uncomfortable in my father's world.

"Would you like something to drink?" He smiled. "I suppose I should ask how old you are."

"Twenty-four."

"You like scotch?"

"No."

"Bourbon perhaps?"

I didn't respond. He poured us both a drink, handed me mine, then sat down across from me. He took a drink and nodded.

It was very good bourbon. Of course it was. I held the taste on tongue. I still needed a cigarette.

I watched Richard Fry walk to his desk, pick up the phone and call his secretary. She came into the room. He smiled at her, gave her a folder and told her she could leave for the day. She liked him—that was obvious. He liked her back. That too was obvious.

She smiled at me as she was walking out the door. "Don't let Richard give you more than two of those. If he offers you a third, excuse yourself or call the cops."

Richard laughed.

We sat in silence for a few seconds.

"She's great," he said.

I nodded.

"I represented her years ago," he said.

"Really?" That interested me. "She didn't kill anyone, did she?"

"Almost," he said. "She was a stripper. She stabbed a guy who tried to rape her."

"Good for her," I said.

"My sentiments exactly."

"So you just hired her?"

"Yeah, something like that. My former legal secretary trained her, showed her the ropes. She went to school in the evenings. Then one day my secretary tells me she's moving to Florida. Mariana took over my office. Don't know what I'd do without her."

"So, I take it you got her off."

"Yeah, well, it wasn't that difficult a case."

I took another drink. "So, you're like this fucking saint or what?"

He smiled, then looked down at the floor, then looked up at me again. "Sometimes decent people make you do decent things. There's nothing extraordinary about that, Charlie."

I didn't want to like him but I did. Still, the expensive suit bothered me. And the manicured fingernails. I stopped myself from taking a sip from my bourbon.

He swished his drink around, then dipped his finger into his glass and stirred it. "I guess you're wondering why you're here."

"I'm always wondering why I'm here—no matter where I am."

He studied me, my face, my hands, my eyes.

"I handled most of your father's legal matters."

I nodded. "You're an interesting choice."

"He was looking for a new attorney. He gave me my first break."

"That surprises me. You're nothing like him."

"I wasn't a part of his world. He wanted someone who didn't have competing interests."

"You're nothing like him," I repeated.

He nodded. "Not that you'd know."

I nodded back at him. "Yeah, not that I'd know."

We were both trying to hide our smiles.

"You and your father weren't close." It wasn't a question.

"My father hated me."

"Yes, I think he did."

I don't know why that made me laugh.

"Love wasn't his strong suit, Charlie."

"Not my strong suit either."

"Well, at least he left you a fortune."

I didn't know what to do with that information. I don't know what he saw on my face.

He repeated it. "He left you a fortune."

"Why would he do something like that?"

"Your father was a complicated man."

"I suppose he was. But who isn't?"

He was studying me again. "You look like your mother."

"That's not my fault."

It was his turn to laugh.

"I don't want his money," I said.

"I'm going to give you some advice."

"I have a therapist for that."

"Take the money, Charlie."

"Give it to my mother."

"The last thing your mother needs is more money."

"Taking his money will only make me hate myself more."

He was very quiet for a moment. "Then hate yourself in comfort."

I didn't laugh at his joke.

"Take the money, Charlie. Do some good with it."

"Yeah, well, why don't you do that for me?"

For an instant, it seemed as though he'd left the room. And then he came back. "Your father actually left the money to you and your brother. To the both of you." He looked at me. "I have something to tell you, Charlie."

I knew what he was going to say.

He rubbed his forefinger over his bottom lip. "I have some bad news."

I didn't say anything. I waited for him to just say it.

"It's about your brother."

I nodded.

We looked at each other.

"I'm sorry," he whispered. "I know how much you loved him."

I downed my drink. "How would you know that?" I could hear the anger in my own voice.

He took the drink from my hand, walked to where he kept his liquor and poured us both another drink.

He handed me my drink, then sat back down. I could feel myself trembling. The bourbon burned in my throat. I could tell he was almost as lost as I was—and wondered why. "What do you know about my brother?" There was still that anger in my voice.

"I knew him."

"What does that mean, you knew him?"

"I used to send him money—when he needed it."

"Where? Where was he living?"

"Buenos Aires."

"And you sent him money?"

"Yes. When he needed it."

"Your money or my father's money?"

"You have to ask that?"

"Why would you send him money?"

"Because I have too much of it. And he had nothing."

"Why would he get in touch with you?"

"Because—" He stopped. "I liked your brother, Charlie. I was a very young attorney when I met him. He worked for me one summer when he was seventeen."

I knew before he told me. Just by the look on his face. "You liked my brother? Or loved him?"

He looked away from me. "I didn't know I was that transparent. I'm going to have to do something about that before I go to court next week." He looked at me, his eyes on mine. "Yes," he whispered. "I loved him."

"Did he love you back?"

"He was so young, Charlie, he was so, so young."

"But did he love you?"

"Yes. He loved me."

"My father never knew?"

"Do you think I'd still be his attorney if he'd have known?"

I didn't know what to say.

Richard shook his head. "I wish I would have been a braver man."

"Are you braver now?" I asked.

"I don't know."

I took a sip from my drink. Then another. "How did he die?"

"His lover killed him. You want the details?"

I shrugged.

"His lover was an addict."

I didn't say anything.

"And, well, one night—"

"Stop. I don't care. I don't want to know."

He nodded. I wondered if I looked as sad as he did. He wanted to explain, to talk, so I let him. "When your father died, I tried to contact Antonio. I couldn't reach him. I hired a detective in Buenos Aires to find him. It didn't take him long to come back to me with the news."

I placed my hands over my face. I don't know how long I sat there and cried. Richard didn't try to comfort me. He just sat there quietly and let me cry for as long as I needed to. It was strange, to feel pain. I'd lost Antonio so long ago. So why did it still hurt? I finished my drink. I looked at my watch. "Shit," I said. "I have the early shift today."

"What do you do?" Richard's voice was soft.

"I'm a part-time student." I looked down at the floor. "And I'm a bartender."

"An honorable profession."

"I don't know about that. It's just serving people drinks."

"We all serve people what they want. You could say I'm just a more expensive bartender than you are."

I couldn't read his expression. "You're like him," he said. "You have his eyes. And you have his smile."

"Can I ask you a question?"

"Sure."

"Did you seduce my brother?"

He didn't hesitate when he answered. "No. He seduced me. He made me feel like a boy." There were tears running down his face.

"I'm sorry," I said. "That was a mean thing to ask."

He shook his head. "No. No, it wasn't." He sat so still. I wondered if his heart had stopped beating. I don't know why I thought that. "I let him go," he whispered. "I let your brother go." We both sat there for a long time. I didn't mind the silence. And then I heard him whisper, "Your brother loved you. You do know that, don't you, Charlie?"

I don't know what I said to him. I must have said something. Sometimes I get so tired of remembering what I say to other people. I just don't remember. And I don't care. I do remember leaving his office. I remember walking around downtown El Paso, just walking. I remember telling myself that Antonio was dead. *My brother my brother my brother*. My brother who divorced the English language and got married to another, the language my parents refused to speak. Yeah, yeah, yeah, he died in another language. That's what I thought. That's funny. That's so, so fucking funny.

I found myself back at my apartment, going through my drawers, looking for my passport. I put it in the back pocket of my jeans and found myself walking across the bridge, going into Juárez. No one went there anymore.

Everybody was afraid of getting killed. You know, stray bullets everywhere. Lots of bullets in Juárez. Maybe I'd get lucky and one of those bullets would find me. I don't know. I don't know what I was thinking. I remember the line of soldiers on Avenida Juárez. I walked past them, pretending they weren't there.

I sat at the Kentucky Club and ordered a drink. Then I left and went into the Cucaracha. The Cucaracha was empty. The owner didn't much like gringos. I told him I wasn't a gringo. Told him I hated gringos as much as he did. I sat there and drank myself silly.

I tried to remember my brother's face.

I remember walking back across the bridge. I remember that. I remember sitting at the Tap, getting drunker and drunker. That's all I remember.

I must have done something bad. Something stupid. Something mean. Must have. Because when I woke up, I was in a holding cell. There was blood all over my shirt. There was dry blood on my fists. My head was throbbing like a sonofabitch. *What did I do? What the fuck did I do?* I was thinking that maybe I could call David. But therapists didn't generally bail their patients out of jail. Then I thought of Richard. That was his department. That's who I could call. But then I thought, *screw it.* Maybe I'll just let myself rot in here.

I thought of Jesús, the bartender I worked with. He asked me once if I'd ever done crack. I said, "No."

"You should try it."

"No, I don't think so. Why would I want to do that shit?"

He smiled at me and said, "It makes you feel alive. Fucking amazing."

I looked at him and said, "Why would anybody want to feel alive?"

I closed my eyes and wondered if I could keep them shut forever.

SOMETIMES THE RAIN

There's always a gun around—even when you can't see it.

There's always a finger that's embedded somewhere in your brain, a finger that's itching to pull the trigger of the gun that's always around.

And when the trigger is pulled, you remember all the shit that ever happened to you: that awful day in second grade when you were in hurry and caught your foreskin in your zipper and had to be rushed to the hospital for an unplanned circumcision; that winter night when Rose slapped you again and again and again until your lip was bleeding, slapped you, yelled at you, kicked you, cussed at you—and all this for delivering the news that her husband had died in an accident; the time your father whispered that you were no good—even as he lay on his death bed.

It could happen anytime. The finger tightens, pulls, and a bullet goes flying through the air. That's how remembering is. The gun, the trigger, the itchy finger, the bullet: a CD playing as I drove on a lonely road in New Mexico, Louie Armstrong singing a song about summer, about fish jumping and swimming holes and fishing poles—and me nodding, lipping the words, not really singing, just lipping. And then the rain pouring down. That's when the bullet went shooting right through me.

And there he was. Brian Stillman.

I'd never been one for having my picture taken. I always managed to skip school on picture day. I was something of a recidivist truant. The yearbook always had this dumb cartoon in place of my picture that said *Gone fishing*. When I entered high school in 1967, I was fifteen years old, looked ten, acted like I was thirteen. I hated myself because I looked like a little boy and wanted to look like a man, wanted to look like the guys who were advanced, not mentally, hell, the guys that were physically advanced and already shaving, hell, they didn't know shit about thinking. And thinking was the last thing they were interested in. Some of those guys who looked like men in junior high school, they didn't start thinking until they were in their thirties. By then it was too late. But I still wanted to look like them.

Brian Stillman, he was one of those physically advanced guys. He must have been shaving since he was in sixth grade. And he could've been one of those guys who didn't start thinking until it was too late. But he wasn't.

I'd known him since entering high school. He was in some of my classes. And we were both on the cross-country team. I hated sports and hated guys who played them. I didn't fit in with Brian Stillman and all his buddies, didn't fit in with the coaches and their attitudes. But running wasn't a sport to me. Running was a place—the only place where I belonged.

There was no reason in the universe that I should have ever known anything about Brian Stillman. Except that something happened. I guess that about sums up living. Something always happens.

It was April of 1970 and we were weeks away from graduation. I'd finally grown three or four inches and all my pimples had disappeared. I could actually bear to look at myself in the mirror. I was trying to decide if I was good looking or not. I hated that it mattered so much.

It was a Thursday and I had decided to skip school. I don't know why, not that I needed a reason. Maybe it's because I had my parent's car that day. I got to drive to school a couple of times a week—when my mom carpooled to the factory. My dad, he had a beat-up Studebaker truck. Painted it blue. Looked nice, drove like shit—and he never let me touch it. "It's a piece of shit, anyway," I told him once when he didn't let me drive it.

"That piece of shit is worth more than you are." That about summed up my father's opinion of me.

So that day, I had the car. A white Chevy Impala, twelve years old. I'd lost my wallet and my license along with it. I hadn't made the time to get a new one. My father told me I was the worst driver ever to get behind a wheel. "You're fucking gonna die in a crash. Won't live to be thirty." But my parents had bigger worries than letting me drive their car. My oldest brother was in the can—ten years for robbing a 7-Eleven with a weapon. My parents insisted he was set up. I knew better. My oldest brother was the meanest sonofabitch I'd ever met. I would never have used the word *innocent* within ten feet of him. My sister, two years younger, was pregnant and living with my grandmother. My youngest brother died of meningitis. My father's grief and disappointment turned to rage. The rage was pointed in my direction. Hell, me driving without a license didn't even register on the list of things my parents were worried about.

I lit a cigarette and sped away from the school parking lot and made good my escape. I hated fourth, fifth and sixth periods. I was acing all the classes. So why go? The rent-a-cop didn't even notice I was driving off campus without a pass. He was too busy flirting with a girl who would land him in the same place as my brother if he wasn't careful.

I didn't have a plan. Anywhere but school. School was hell. I felt like an ice cube that was slowly, slowly melting. I felt if I stayed in that school one more second, I would disappear. The sad part was that nobody would notice.

I drove around town. Not much going on at one thirty in the afternoon. I always thought Las Cruces, New Mexico, took a siesta in the afternoons. On certain days, I was convinced the town didn't even bother to wake up.

I wound up at the river—which was everyone's favorite place to go, a place where you could get drunk or get stoned and put in an eight-track tape and listen to Janis Joplin sing those great songs which were angry and sad and rough and beautiful. Someone else's pain was always beautiful. And after that tape was done, you could pop it out and put in *Abbey Road* and listen to it over and over again. I memorized every word of "She Came In Through the Bathroom Window."

I parked the car and listened to Janis Joplin. I sat there on the hood of my car and smoked cigarettes and stared out at the water and the sky and I thought that this was as close as I was ever going to get to heaven.

And then I noticed Brian standing there. It was as if he just appeared. "Hey," he said, "can I bum a smoke?"

"Sure," I said. Like we were friends.

We sat there on the hood of my car and smoked.

"She broke up with me," he said.

I looked at him. "Bummer," I said. I don't think we'd actually ever spoken to each other. We probably said *Hi* or something like *How's it hangin'*. The thing was that I hung out with guys like me—Mexicans who went to school because they had to and who mostly had jobs after school and on weekends. Brian hung out with guys like him—gringos who belonged to the Future

Farmers of America and wore blue corduroy jackets and thought they owned the school. They *did* own the school. So what? They could have it.

I think he was waiting for me to say something else besides *bummer.* "So you still like her?"

"I don't know," he said. He sort of laughed. "She's pretty, you know? But her name's Beth," he said.

I don't know why I thought that was funny, but I found myself laughing. So we sat there and laughed.

We smoked. We talked, not a lot. Brian wasn't a talker. I was. I really liked talking. Talking and sleeping, those were my two favorite things. But I didn't have much to say, not to Brian Stillman.

I could see the guy was lost. One thing was for sure—he'd lost his ride back into town.

"So you got dumped."

"Pretty much. I think I wanted her to dump me. And it's not as if I was gonna marry her." He took a puff from his cigarette. "You still hanging out with Rosie?" I didn't know he knew anything about my life.

"Nah. Rosie's history."

"Too bad. She's fine."

Rosie *was* fine. And she'd been right to give me the highway. What was she doing with a guy like me? I lit another cigarette.

He looked at his watch. "School's almost out."

"Yeah."

"I hate school," he said.

"Brian Stillman hates school? Could have fooled me."

"Why? I'm not smart. Not like you."

"I'm not so fucking smart."

"How many A's you have on that report card?"

"So what?"

"You understand things, Neto."

It was funny to hear him call me Neto. Most gringos just called me Ernie. "I'm not sure I'm getting you."

"How do you do it? The teacher calls on you and you always answer as if you wrote the fucking book."

That made me laugh.

"How'd you learn how to think?"

"I don't know. I go to a lot of movies."

That really made him laugh. He flicked his cigarette. "So, you goin' to college?"

"Yeah. Sure. Why the hell not?"

"Well, there's always the army."

"The army's never gonna own my ass. And that's the fucking truth."

"Well, I've kinda thought about joining."

I looked him and shook my head. "There's a war going on, Stillman. Anybody let you in on that dirty little secret?"

"I might get drafted."

"Not if you go to college."

He nodded. "Maybe I just need to get out of here."

I nodded. "I get that."

"You should leave too, Neto," he said. "You're too good for this fucking place."

Yeah, too good. Like that was true. We smoked another cigarette together.

I offered him a ride home. He lived on a farm just off Highway 478. His house was about half a mile in from the road. We didn't talk that much as we drove along. Just listened to *Abbey Road*. He pointed. "This is my stop. I'll walk the rest of the way."

"I can take you all the way in," I said.

"Nah. My old man—" he stopped in mid-sentence. "He's a piece of work." He had this real sad look on his face. I wished to God I hadn't seen that look. It made me like him. He opened the door and started to get out of the car. But then he just sat back down on the seat. "You still run, Neto?"

"Yeah, I still run."

"So why'd you quit the team?"

"Cross-country wasn't my thing."

"You were the best runner. That's why they hated you. They could never beat you."

I nodded. *Yeah, sure, they could never beat me.*

"You should have stayed on the team."

"I wasn't having a good time."

"Well," he said. "We sure as fuck made sure of that, didn't we?" He got out of the car. Then he put his head through the window. "I'm sorry I was such an asshole," he said.

"It doesn't matter," I said.

"Yeah," he said, "it *does* matter, Neto." He flipped me a peace sign, then shut the door.

I watched him walk down the dirt road lined by pecan trees along a ditch.

I thought about how sad he looked as I drove off. I thought of all the time I'd wasted hating him.

The next night, I was going out. Friday night, on the cusp of summer and graduation and manhood. Yeah, going out. Just some guys who wanted to head out to a keg party at the river, maybe meet a girl and kiss her. *And* if you were lucky, she'd kiss you back. And you might feel something inside of you. Maybe that's why we went to the river.

School was ending and maybe, *just maybe*, life was beginning. I'd applied to State and got accepted. That surprised me. I even got a two thousand dollar scholarship, which was a fortune. But I'd also applied to the University of New Mexico in Albuquerque. They'd given me the exact same scholarship. Not that Albuquerque was worlds away, but it was far enough. I hadn't told anyone, not even my parents. I wasn't sure what to do, but I didn't want their advice. I wanted to make a decision that was all mine. I kept pinching myself. Me, Ernesto Zaragoza—I was going to college. I was thinking about all those things while I waited for José and Jimmy to pick me up.

My mom and dad were sitting on the front porch, my father reading the newspaper, my mother reading (or praying) her novena. "*No te pongas marijuano, cabron.*" My father shot me his favorite look. The man could scare me in two languages. Talented guy, my father.

José drove up in his father's jeep. I kissed my mom and smiled at my dad. "I'll be good, Dad." I always said that to him. It pissed him off when I said things like that. He didn't actually want me to be a good boy. He wanted me to be a man. But a man who didn't smoke marijuana. For him that was the worst.

José and Jimmy waved at my mom and dad. My mom was all smiles. My dad scowled. José got a big kick out of my dad. I never really knew why. Like scowling was something amusing.

There were about five or six keg parties at the river. Five or six or seven or eight. José was looking for one in particular. His cousin Mike was hosting him and his buddies. José pointed as he drove. "That's Mike's truck." We pulled up in front of the crowd, got out of the jeep and did the shaking-hands business, the casual hugs that we learned from watching our fathers. Yeah, like we were men. But you had to hug in just the right way and always slap the other guy on the back. That's how it worked.

I got handed a beer.

The sun was setting and there was a breeze and everything was so perfect. I felt almost happy. I don't really remember much about Mike's keg party. Rosie arrived along with a group of about six girls. Then another group of girls arrived. Girls always arrived in packs. It was protection. That's how I thought about it. It made me sad to think that they needed it. Protection from guys like us.

Rosie and I talked. She was so pretty. I mean, pretty in ways that most girls envied. She was real. Sometimes, I wanted to just keep looking at her. "You should leave this town," she said.

"Are you chasing me out?"

She laughed. She kissed me on the cheek. "I like you, you idiot."

"Then how come you broke up with me?"

"Because we're just friends. There something wrong with that?"

"Guess not," I said. "Still, maybe I'm a little insulted."

"Don't be. I don't want boyfriends. I want to go to college and get a life. A life that's mine."

"A life that's all yours, huh?"

She laughed. "It sounds beautiful, doesn't it, Neto?"

And then I found myself laughing my ass off. "Yeah, Rosie, it sure does sound beautiful."

She smiled. She looked like an angel. "I'm going to U.T."

"Austin? No shit?"

"No shit."

"Scholarship?"

"The works, Neto."

"I'm fucking impressed."

"I should thank you."

"For what?"

"Remember when we were in junior high?"

"What are you talking about?"

"You used to read to me."

"I almost forgot about that."

"It did something to me. There were other worlds out there. And you knew that. And you wanted me to know that too."

She smiled at me. It broke my heart, her smile.

I lit a cigarette. She took the cigarette away from me and took a puff. She kissed me on the cheek. "Don't forget to write." And just like that, she walked away.

I guess I didn't feel much like partying. Maybe there was something wrong with me. I had a few beers, mostly listened to people talking a lot of bullshit. Some guy tried to put his arm around Rosie. She grabbed his paw and shoved it aside. "Go wash your hands," she said.

I smiled. She noticed I was watching. She smiled back at me. Rosie didn't need anybody to take care of her. That's what I liked about her.

Some guys lit a bonfire. It was getting dark and the weather was perfect and I *really was* almost happy.

I walked away and headed to another keg party. I knew some people there, not people I hung with, but you know, school friends. We shot the shit, talked about some crazy things that had happened during high school. Everyone remembered when the gym got spray-painted asking the principal to suck everyone's cock. Nice. Yeah, well, it was high school. There was a lot of laughing. I felt alone. And didn't mind it. It was one of those things, feeling alone. Sometimes it was better than being with other people.

I lit a cigarette and decided to go off and sit by the river. Think about things. I liked thinking about things. My mom called it daydreaming. My dad said I was lazy. They were both wrong. I wasn't daydreaming and the lazy thing, well, my brain didn't have a lazy cell in its body.

I don't know how long I walked, but I was pretty far from all the bonfires. I went and found a good spot by the river where I could take off my shoes. I lay down on the bank, my feet in the water, the stars in the sky. I thought for a second that maybe my life would be a good one. And I would go through life this happy, happy guy. And then, in the middle of all that happy conversation I was having with myself, I heard something. I didn't know what it was, at first, and so I made myself perfectly still and listened. I knew the sound. Someone was having sex. I mean they were really having sex. I smiled to myself. Yeah, someone was getting lucky as hell. I knew I was being a voyeur or something but what was I supposed to do at that point? So I just sat there and listened.

Whoever they were, they were having a good time. A better time than I'd ever had. And then there it was, the point of all the sex, the climax. Why did people always say, *god, god, god* when they came? I was smiling my ass off. But then I realized something. Something that really confused me. There was no girl. The voices were talking now, and both voices, well, they were both guys. I just kept listening. "I might love you," one of the voices said.

And the other voice said, "Don't love me."

"It's too late, Brian."

"Jorge, you know—I mean—I don't know what I mean."

"You're the one who started this. Now it's too late."

"It's not too late."

"You want to pretend that nothing's going on between us?"

"No, no, that's not what I mean."

"Then what, Brian?"

"I don't know what I mean."

They were starting to get mad at each other. My heart was beating fast and I wanted to just get out of there, but I knew they'd hear me and I didn't want them to know I was there. I felt confused but I knew, I knew who they were, God, I knew them. It was Brian Stillman and Jorge Ledesma. Jorge lived on Brian's farm. His dad had come from Mexico to work with the Stillman's. Jorge was quiet and tall and had the body of an athlete. But not from working out, just from working on the Stillman farm. In grade school I'd helped him learn English. But we had never been friends. I don't know why. Maybe it was because I wasn't good at making friends. Maybe it was because I'd been an asshole and didn't want to hang around with Mexican Mexicans. I mean, maybe I wanted to be an American. Hell, I don't remember. We just weren't friends.

I kept listening even though I didn't want to listen. I tried looking up at the stars, tried concentrating on them, but I could still hear everything. And then I heard Brian say, "If I don't leave this goddamn place, I'm gonna go nuts."

"Why?" I could tell Jorge was crying. "Why are you leaving?"

"I can't stay here. I can't." And then there was this long silence. "You can come with me, Jorge."

"My mom's sick, Brian. I can't leave her."

"You need a life. *I* need a life."

"You hate your father."

"*He* hates me, Jorge. And I'm not fucking staying."

"And what about me?"

And then there was nothing. Nothing at all.

My heart was beating really fast. And I felt—I really don't know how I felt. I just lay there, my feet in the water, unable to light a cigarette, waiting for them to leave. And then I heard them moving. And then I heard Brian's voice. "Hey, hey, don't. Don't be sad. We'll figure something out." I pictured Jorge leaning into Brian's shoulder. I pictured Brian's arms around Jorge. I didn't know why I was picturing those things.

I heard them walking away.

They were talking again, saying things, but their voices were distant now, and then their voices disappeared.

I lit a cigarette. I looked up at the stars. And suddenly the world was so much bigger than I'd ever imagined it to be. And I couldn't get the idea of Brian kissing Jorge out of my brain.

I had them both in my head when I masturbated that night.

I was trembling.

I knew something about myself that I'd never known. Just when I'd started liking myself, I hated myself again.

The day after graduation, I decided I was going to college in Albuquerque. I told my dad. I don't know why I thought he might actually be proud of me. "Think you're smart enough?"

"I got a scholarship, Dad."

"You'll be back after you fuck that up." That's all he had to say.

My mom cried. "Your father doesn't mean it," she said.

She needed my smile. "I know," I said. We both knew it wasn't true. But we needed to lie to ourselves and to each other about the truth of who my father was. What could a woman tell herself when she knew what kind of man she'd married? What could a guy tell himself about a father who'd never love him? It was easier to smile.

I worked two jobs that summer. Saved money. The scholarship gave me two thousand dollars up front and paid my tuition for the first year. The letter said if I kept up my grades, then the scholarship would be renewed for another year. After that, I was on my own. That was a lot. God, that was so much money. A fortune. But still I knew it wouldn't be enough. And I was already thinking about the last two years and how I would pay for that. And I kept telling myself this one thing: *I am not going to be poor.* I knew I'd have to do it on my own. So it was me and work. Hell, I knew how to do that. I was living for the future. I guess I'd always been doing that.

I didn't really hang out with anybody that summer. I was too tired. I'd work on a construction site from six in the morning till three in the afternoon. I'd come home, take a shower, eat, relax and go into work at the 7-Eleven from five till eleven. Saturdays, I'd work an eight-hour shift at the 7-Eleven. Sundays, I'd just sleep. That was my life. That, and dreaming of my new life in Albuquerque.

One Saturday afternoon in July, I decided I needed to do something besides read a book or watch television. My parents were out of town at a funeral in San Diego. They'd let me stay behind so I could work. I liked having the house to myself—not that it really felt like home. My dad had a way of making sure I knew that the house I lived in was *his.*

But being alone was really good. Really, really good.

I decided I'd find some beer or something. The needing-to-feel-alive thing. Yeah, that was always there. I went riding around, smoking cigarettes, felt kinda lost and kinda sad but didn't know why. I guess I hated my life. I found some homeless guy and he was asking for money. I told him to buy me a six-pack and I'd give him a couple of bucks. He was hungry to take the bait. We both got what we wanted. "God bless you, son," he said.

I shook my head. "Let's leave God out of this one."

I drove around. I don't know why, but I found myself taking the old farm road. I liked that road. I'd grown up on a farm before my father lost it. He lost it betting on a cock fight. Yeah, well, that was my father. I hated him when we had to move. But I'd never hated him as much as he hated me. I just didn't have it in me. I wondered if deep down he wanted to love me as much as I wanted to love him. But there were certain things you couldn't do anything about. Fathers were one of those certain things.

So there I was on Highway 478. Driving down the road, smoking a cigarette. And then I saw him. Brian Stillman. At first I wasn't sure if it was him, but as I drove closer I knew it *was* him. It *was*. He was all beat-up to shit. I mean, the guy's face was all bloody and he was just stumbling around, like he'd gone ten rounds. Goddamn, I thought. He'd taken off his T-shirt and was using it as a giant handkerchief for his bloody nose. I stopped the car by the side of the road and yelled his name. "Brian!" He looked at me. He was numb. He just stood there staring at me. Then he just waved me away.

"Brian?"

He waved me away again.

"Get in the car," I said.

He shook his head.

I got out of the car and grabbed him by the arm. "You're hurt," I said. "Get in the car."

"Don't call anyone," he said.

"I won't. You need help."

"Fuck you, Neto."

"Don't give me that fuck you shit. That's not gonna work on me. Just get in the car."

He was too tired and too beat-up and too sad to fight me. He got in the car and stared out the window. I handed him a beer. "Here."

He took it. He chugged down the whole thing. And then he just started crying. I didn't say anything.

"Just don't tell anyone," he said. And then he was crying again.

"Who am I gonna tell?"

After a while, he stopped sobbing but the quiet tears kept running down his face.

"You need to get cleaned up," I said. "Maybe you need to see a doctor."

"No way," he said. "No fucking doctors."

I thought he was going to hit me. "Okay, okay," I said. I handed him a cigarette. He was trembling as he smoked. I kept watching him out of the corner of my eye.

I drove toward my house, neither one of us saying anything.

When we got to my neighborhood, Brian looked at me. "Where are we going?"

"My house," I said.

"I don't want—"

"My parents are out of town," I said. "It's okay."

He didn't say anything.

When we got to my house, I had to help him get out of the car. I thought he really needed to see a doctor. But I knew Brian wasn't going to go for that.

I helped him to the couch and handed him another beer. He drank this one slowly. He wasn't shaking as much. I gave him a cigarette and then went looking for a wet towel. His lip was cut but it had stopped bleeding. I could tell someone had taken a fist to his handsome face.

I handed him a wet washcloth. "Here," I said. He tried his best to clean himself up. I knew he was hurting. I'd been in a couple of fights. Not a smart thing for a guy to do when he wasn't a fighter.

"Who did this to you, Brian?"

He looked at me. I guess he'd decided he could trust me. "My father," he whispered.

Great, I thought. But I didn't say anything. I just kept staring at his beat-up face. "He's a fuck," I said.

He almost smiled when I said that.

"Why?" I said. "Why did he do that to you? He's a fuck."

He shook his head. I knew he wasn't going to tell me.

And then I said, "Hell, it doesn't matter why. You don't deserve that."

"He hates me." He started crying again. I hated to see him like that, like a dog that's been kicked around. God, I hated that. I almost wanted to cry too.

"My dad hates me too," I said. "Maybe our dads went to the same father school."

He smiled. I was glad he could still smile.

"Are you sure you don't want to go to a doctor?"

"I don't think anything's broken."

"You sure?"

He shrugged.

"You're gonna have a helluva shiner. Shit, Brian, *two* shiners."

He shrugged again.

"You don't deserve this, Brian." I wanted to shove that phrase into his heart. But I knew he'd always believe that he did deserve what he got. I somehow understood that.

"Maybe I do," he said.

I shook my head.

I helped him get to the shower. I could hear him groan as he washed himself. I lent him some clothes. He was bigger than me but my T-shirts fit him and I found a pair of my father's jeans that fit him.

He looked so sad and small sitting there, even though he wasn't small at all. I gave him some aspirin and some ice to put on his shiner. We drank a beer together. "Why are you doing this?" he asked me.

"Doing what?"

"Helping me."

"Because I'm not your father and I don't hate you."

"You should hate me," he said. "I was always an asshole around you."

"It didn't kill me."

"If you really knew me, I think you'd hate me."

"Maybe I do know you," I said.

He looked at me. "Nobody knows me."

I wanted to say *Jorge knows you*. But I didn't. I thought I should just let it go.

He fell asleep on the couch.

I watched him sleep.

I knew what I thought as I watched him sleep even though I didn't really want to tell myself what I thought. I thought he was beautiful. I didn't let myself tell myself. But I did think he was beautiful.

He slept all afternoon, and then at night I let him sleep on my bed. I slept on the couch and read a book. I couldn't sleep.

In the morning, I made breakfast. We didn't talk much.

He offered to wash the dishes. I let him. He wanted to do something for me. Yeah, I let him wash the dishes.

He wasn't crying anymore. And he wasn't trembling. But his face, God, it was swollen. We hung out that day. It was Sunday, my only day off and I had no plans. And Brian had nowhere to go.

"Your mom won't worry about you?"

"I doubt it," he said. "She died when I was eight."

"I didn't know," I said.

"She loved me," he said.

I nodded. We hung out. I kept making him put ice on his face. But since it was Sunday, we couldn't get any beer. We broke into my father's liquor cabinet. I pulled out a nearly full bottle of Jack Daniels.

"Won't your father kill you for that?"

I smiled. I marked the bottle with a magic marker. "Tomorrow, I'll get one of the guys on the construction site to buy me a bottle. And I'll replace it. Easy."

"You smile a lot," he said.

"Do I?"

He was going to say something else—but he didn't. We drank Jack and coke and smoked cigarettes. Brian kept feeling his face and wincing. He looked sad and I tried to talk about stuff that didn't matter very much. Songs we liked. Our favorite movies.

After a few Jack and cokes, we were feeling pretty good.

Brian looked at me and said, "I kinda envy you."

"First time I've ever heard that one," I said.

"You have a lot of friends, Neto."

"No, I don't. Not a lot."

"Everyone likes you."

That made me laugh. "That's because no one knows me."

He smiled. I was glad his father hadn't broken any of his teeth. "We're the same," he said.

And then we both just laughed.

We talked about other stuff, but we didn't talk about girls. I think most guys would have wound up talking about girls. But we didn't. And I knew there was a reason for that. I didn't want to think about the reason.

We decided to go to a drive-in movie that night. But then, on the way to the drive-in, I looked over at Brian and said, "Hey, let's go to Juárez."

He smiled.

I smiled back. "It'll be fun."

"You mean we'll get smashed."

"Yeah, I guess." I started laughing. I was thinking that maybe going to Juárez for a night on the town would make us both feel alive. "I have money in my wallet," I said. And just like that we were down the freeway headed for the border that was forty miles away. We didn't talk much as we drove. We smoked cigarette after cigarette and listened to the radio and both of us sang along and I noticed he had a nice voice, could carry a tune, and for a few moments nothing was wrong—nothing at all. When we got to the bridge, I parked the car at one of the parking lots and paid the attendant a couple of dollars. We paid two cents apiece to cross the Santa Fe Bridge and as we walked across, I felt my heart racing. I always felt that way when I went to Juárez. It was something that I wasn't allowed to do. And yet, all through high school, I'd always managed to make my way there with my friends. But tonight felt different. There was thunder in the summer sky and lightning in the distance and I knew the rain was coming and I wanted to reach over and touch Brian and say something to him. Something that mattered. But what could a guy like me say to a guy like Brian that would matter?

"Jorge and I used to come to the bars here sometimes."

"Yeah?" I said.

"Yeah. We got drunk one time and then ate some tacos from a street vendor. Best tacos I ever had."

When we stepped out on Avenida Juárez, I looked at Brian and laughed. "So—lots of bars. Take your pick."

He didn't skip a beat. "The Kentucky Club," he said.

I was going to suggest a place called The Cave. A real dive. I liked it. But hell, I didn't care. "Sounds good," I said.

"It was my mother's favorite place," Brian whispered.

"Really?"

"Not that I really know. It's just that this one time, my father was drunk and he said, 'If your mother was still alive, I'd take her to the Kentucky Club. She loved that place. I'd walk over to the jukebox and play all the Frank Sinatra tunes they had. Your mother knew all the words.' That's the only time he ever said anything about my mother after she died."

I thought he was going to cry. "I'm sorry about your mother," I said.

"I'm tired of being sorry," he said. "I'm so fucking tired."

The Kentucky Club wasn't far. When we walked in, the place was half-full but there were two seats at the bar so we claimed them. We sat next to a couple of drunk gringos who were talking about the night Elizabeth Taylor sashayed in after getting a quickie divorce from Eddie Fisher. "She bought everybody in the joint a drink." They talked about that night as if they'd both been there. It's funny how people lie to themselves. But, hell, what was the harm? Brian gave me a nudge with his knee and we smiled and ordered *cuba libres*. I liked the taste of the rum and the coke and liked the feel of sitting at a bar with Brian.

"So this is what it's like," I said.

"What?" Brian said.

"To feel like a man."

Brian laughed. "I think it takes a little more than that."

"Yeah," I said. "I know. I'm just being an asshole."

"You're not," he said. "You're not an asshole."

I nodded. We had another drink. Then another. Then another.

Then Brian looked at me and said, "I could sit here forever."

And I thought, *Me too. So long as you were sitting right next to me.*

I don't know how many drinks we had, but somewhere along the line we decided to call it a night and found ourselves walking across the bridge and saying *American* when the border guard asked us to declare our citizenship. One of the border guys asked Brian if he'd gotten into a fight. Brian just nodded. "Yeah," he said. "No big deal." We made our way to the parking lot that was mostly empty.

When we were back on the freeway, Brian said, "Thanks, Neto."

"For what?" I said.

"For everything."

Everything. I wondered what everything meant. Maybe everything meant *not much* and a few drinks at the Kentucky Club.

I don't know how I managed to drive home that night. But I did. I remember I kept wanting to reach over and touch Brian—just touch him—but I didn't.

I went back to work the next day hungover as hell. Brian stayed at my house. After work, I grabbed a shower and then we went out for a burger. When we paid, Brian took out his wallet. I noticed that all he had was a ten dollar bill.

"I'll pay," I said.

"No," he said. "You've done enough."

I smiled. "All I did was offer you a place to stay for a few days. Big deal. It's not even my house."

"What do you mean, it's not your house?"

"I mean it's my father's house. I'm only a visitor. And if you want to know the fucking truth, I don't feel that welcome."

He nodded. "I know the feeling."

"So what's your plan?" I said. God, his face was still all beat-up. But at least there wasn't any more swelling.

"I guess I'd better come up with something."

I nodded. "Why don't you drop me off at work. You can take the car. Drive around. Think about things."

"You have another job?"

"Yeah, two jobs. I'm saving to go to school."

"I guess I better get me a job too."

"Ever had a job, Brian?"

"I've worked my ass off on the farm my whole life. Guess that doesn't count. I mean, it's not as if I got paid."

"It counts," I said.

I wished to God he'd stop looking so sad.

He dropped me off at work. I was thinking he was going to try to see Jorge. That was just a hunch. When I got off work, Brian was there to pick me up. I don't know why exactly, but I drove toward the river. I parked and we got out and smoked and put our feet in the river and sat on the bank.

"I have to leave," Brian said.

"I guess so," I said. "Where?"

"Well, since I don't have a dime, I guess I'm gonna find some work, save a few bucks—then take off to Denver."

"Denver?"

"I always wanted to go there. Maybe I just want to live where it snows."

"What are you gonna do in the snow?"

"Freeze my ass off. What else?"

That made me smile. "Sounds like a plan. But where are you gonna stay? I mean, without money? You could stay with me—except there's this guy I call Dad."

He laughed. I'm glad he laughed. I felt bad. I hated throwing him out. But my dad, well, he wouldn't go for Brian staying with us.

"I'm sorry," I said. "Maybe you could stay with Jorge and his parents."

He shook his head. "I think my dad half expects me to show up there. So he can throw me off his land." He took a drag off his cigarette. "I don't want to cause Jorge's parents any trouble. They're nice people. They're good to me."

"Well, you have a few days to figure something out. My parents aren't coming home until Friday."

He nodded. He was looking at the water in the river. "I saw him," he whispered.

"Who?" I said. But I knew who he was talking about.

"Jorge."

"So you guys good friends?" I hoped he couldn't hear anything in my voice.

"Yeah. Good friends. He's going with his parents back to Mexico."

"Why? I thought they were citizens by now."

"They are."

"So why are they going back?"

"His mother doesn't want to die here."

"She's that sick?"

He nodded.

"That's sad," I said.

"Yeah, real sad."

"Will he ever come back?"

"Some day, I guess."

So Brian went from sad to sadder. Shit. And I couldn't do anything about it. I don't know what made him do it, but he leaned into me. I put my arm around him. I could have stayed that way forever. I wanted to whisper his name but I didn't. He started crying, so I let him sob into my shoulder. There were so many things in his life for him to cry about. *So let him cry,* I thought. *Let him fucking cry.*

I don't remember talking on the way home. Brian was still crying. I think he'd held in his tears his whole life. I thought he felt safe around me. Maybe that's why he could cry. I think it had been a long time since he felt safe. When we got back to my house, I reached over and touched his shoulder. "It will all work out," I said.

I got to thinking that night. And then it came to me. And I knew what I had to do.

When I got back from work the next day, Brian was sitting on the front porch reading a book. It was starting to thunder. A summer storm was coming up and it smelled like rain.

"I love the rain," I said.

"Me too," he said.

I sat next to him and handed him an envelope.

"What's this?"

"Open it," I said.

For a long time he just stared at the money and the bus ticket to Denver.

"I can't take this," he said.

"Yes, you can."

"No, I can't."

"You can pay me back."

"This is five hundred dollars, Neto."

"I know how much it is," I said.

"I can't take it."

"You have to take it," I said. "This is how you start to live again."

"No, it isn't."

"Yes, it is. You start a new life by letting someone help you."

"You worked so fucking hard for this. Neto—"

"You think you can do this all by yourself?"

He handed the envelope back to me.

"I can join up," he said.

"Don't do that, Brian. That's fucked up. Don't do that. You don't want to do that." I shoved the envelope back in his hand. "Take it," I said. "Don't be an asshole."

He started to argue with me again.

"Shut up," I said. "Just listen." I lowered my voice. "Listen to the rain," I whispered. "Sometimes the rain—"

"Sometimes the rain, what? What, Neto?"

"Just listen."

We stopped talking. It was pouring. It was beautiful and frightening, the power of a summer rain. I could feel the hot earth cooling down. I walked out from the protection of the front porch and held my hands up and smiled. "You see, Brian?"

He laughed. God, he could laugh. No one could take that away from him. He stepped out into the rain with me. And I swear that as we stood there, both of us with our hands stretched out—I swear I could hear the beating of his heart. And I thought, *Wouldn't it be sweet if he reached over and kissed me and we could pretend we were in some goddamned Hollywood movie.*

I called in sick that night at the 7-Eleven. I took Brian to a drug store so he could pick up a razor and soap and toothpaste and all that other stuff he'd need. Then we went to a place called Surplus City. He bought a couple pairs of pants, a couple of shirts, underwear, some socks and a few things.

It was raining like it had never rained before. I wanted the storm to go on forever. As I drove back home, I kept smiling. I didn't love anything more than I loved the rain. Brian kept studying my face and I pretended not to notice. I gave him an old suitcase—and when he'd finished packing, he looked at me. He started to say something. But I stopped him. "Let's get you to the bus station."

"I didn't say goodbye to him," he said.

"You should call him," I said.

I went outside as he went to grab the phone. I didn't want to hear what he and Jorge were saying to each other.

After a while, Brian came outside. "He's going to meet us at the bus station."

"Good," I said.

The bus station was quiet. The Greyhound bus for Denver was arriving from El Paso at nine thirty. The bus would be leaving for Denver at ten. We looked at the schedule and sat outside. The rain had stopped but there was thunder and lightning in the distance and the evening breeze was cool and carried the sweet smell of the desert. I thought I was going to cry.

"I don't know what to say," Brian whispered.

"Get yourself happy, Brian."

He nodded. "What about you?"

"Oh," I said, "I think I'll get myself happy too."

When Jorge showed up at the bus depot, I decided it was a good time to make myself scarce. I waved at Jorge, then walked up to his car and shook his hand. "I'm sorry about your mom," I said.

Maybe I said the wrong thing. He looked like he was going to cry. Tears and rain. That's the way it was for us that night. For Jorge and Brian. And me.

I knew the bus from El Paso was coming at any moment. Jorge and Brian could have a little time to themselves before the bus left for Denver. I was awkward at goodbyes back then. I'm awkward even now, these many years later. I think I looked at Brian and said, "Good luck." Or something idiotic like that. But Brian followed me to my car. He looked at me and said, "You're a good guy, Neto."

I nodded.

"You know, me and Jorge, we—"

I nodded. "I know."

"And you don't care?"

"Maybe I'm like you," I said.

We both looked at each other. I remember the way he looked at me. No one had ever looked at me that way.

Me looking at him. Him looking at me. That's how we left it.

I went home. It was raining again.

I let my tears get lost among the falling drops of rain. Becoming a man didn't feel anything like I thought it was going to feel.

About a year later, my mother forwarded me a letter from Brian Stillman. I saw the postmark. He'd joined the Army. I didn't want to open it. I held it for a long time. There was a money order in the envelope for five hundred dollars and a short note that said:

Dear Neto,

I'm in Da Nang. I wanted to write and tell you that I joined up. Maybe I didn't before because I know how you feel about the whole military thing. Maybe I wanted to feel like a real man. Maybe that's why I joined up, to prove something to myself. I want you to understand, Neto, that I had to do this. I know that you hate this war. I think you're the kind of guy who would hate any war. I just couldn't find myself out there in the world. I don't know how to put myself into words, Neto. I'm not like you.

I think about you sometimes. I should have kissed you. But I was so afraid you wouldn't kiss me back. When I go home again, will you be there? I promise to stop being afraid.

Love, Brian

So many things we don't do because we're afraid.

His note made me sad. Crazy man. Crazy, crazy man. What are you doing in Vietnam?

I bought some serious art supplies with that five hundred dollars. I was on my way to becoming an artist and nothing was going to stop me. Not even all my self-doubt. I wrote to Brian and told him I might love him as much as I loved the rain.

I don't know if he ever got the letter. He was killed trying to save one of his buddies in a village somewhere between Da Nang and the Cambodian border.

My mother called and told me there was a picture of him in the newspaper. I couldn't bring myself to go to his funeral. Someone would hand his father a flag and say, *From a grateful nation.* Finally, the sonofabitch would be proud of his son.

For many days I woke with the bitter taste of regret in my mouth.

I was home for a few weeks the summer after I graduated. I was on my way to art school at Columbia University. My father was dying so I came back to spend the summer. It didn't feel like home anymore. It never had.

One evening, I walked to the 7-Eleven to buy a pack of cigarettes. As I stood outside opening my pack of cigarettes, there he was. Just standing there. Jorge. It's funny how people just appear in front of you sometimes. I was buying cigarettes and he was driving around and stopped to buy a coke. That's how it happens.

I wanted to hug him. I offered him a smile and a handshake instead. We had a beer at the river. He asked me how I knew about him and Brian. I told him the story of that night. He laughed. "Nothing is ever as private as you think it is."

I asked him if he'd gone to the funeral.

"I had to."

"Did you see his father?"

"Yes."

"If I would have gone to the funeral, I would have taken my fists to him."

Jorge smiled. "I wanted to tell him that I had once loved his son."

"And did you tell him?"

"No. But he knew."

"Did you ever write to Brian?"

"No. We talked on the phone before he left for 'Nam. We decided to go our own ways. It hurt too much to hang on—at least for me. We were boys together. I don't think we knew how to be men together." He sipped on his beer. "My mom died four months after we got back to Mexico. I moved to California. My father came back here. He said it was home now."

I nodded.

He looked at me. "I think he fell in love with you."

"I doubt it," I said.

"Don't doubt it, Neto. I knew him." He touched my shoulder. "Someday you're going to stop beating up on yourself."

"Someday," I said.

I went home that night and thought of Brian Stillman. I dreamed about him. When I kissed his body, it tasted like the rain.

My father died a few days later. As I sat on his deathbed, he looked up at me. "An artist?" he said. "You'll never be anything." He laughed. He was dying and he laughed. I suppose it's true what they say—that you die the way you lived.

I think it matters very much whether your father loves you or not. Jorge's father had loved him, had never stopped loving him. It showed. Brian's father hadn't loved him. That showed too.

And me? My father hadn't loved me either.

So why did I still cry at his funeral?

I didn't think I would ever return to the desert, but there was something of the landscape that lived in me and so I came back to live in New Mexico. It was good for my painting.

I hadn't thought of Brian Stillman for many years. It was almost as if he'd disappeared from my memory.

My boyhood had been a painful country. I rarely visited that place.

But then one day there was that Louie Armstrong song on an old CD. And it was raining. The gun, the trigger, the finger.

The rain was magnificent in its rage.

I half-expected to turn and see Brian sitting next to me, inconsolable tears running down his face. I stopped the car on the side of the road and stepped out into the rain. I stuck my hands out like a thirsty boy trying to catch all the drops. I shouted out his name to the deaf and angry sky, *Brian Stillman! Brian Stillman! Brian Stillman!*

It was almost like a song.

CHASING THE DRAGON

I have a black and white photograph of my mother and father sitting in a Juárez bar. My father looks like he's drunk, his white shirt wrinkled, his striped tie loosened, his black hair tussled. It amazes me that even in a drunken state, my father retains a charm that could be captured by a camera. My mother, an ethereal beauty with piercing green eyes, is looking away, staring off into the distance. Neither of them appears to be happy.

My parents—in and out of photographs—were an arresting couple. People envied them. They walked into rooms and turned heads. I suspect they enjoyed their public performances. The minute they stepped out into the public eye, they were celebrities, the center of the spinning world. Their physical beauty aside, they lived tortured, miserable lives.

With an authority that only her voice could convey, my aunt Lucille once told me that the picture was taken at the Hawaiian. "Your mother loved that place. She loved the décor, the mai tais and the bartender. Your father hated that hellhole. He thought it was cheap and charmless." Then she reluctantly handed me back the photograph. "Conrad, I don't know what possesses you to keep that picture." My uncle Louie, whose only regret in life was that he would never have the courage to divorce Lucille, the woman he married, pulled me aside and said, "Conrad, that picture was taken at the Kentucky Club. The Hawaiian closed years before that picture was taken." My uncle Louie was addicted to pulling me aside and whispering his versions of family history into my ears. It was his way of making me his co-conspirator. Not that I ever trusted or believed him.

My other uncle, Hector, who was as unreliable as all the rest of the adults in my family, informed me that the picture was taken after my mother caught my father with another woman. "After that, she refused to let him step foot into the Kentucky Club."

"Why?" I asked.

"It was his favorite bar."

"Oh," I said. I think it's safe to say that everyone in my family was more interested in punitive measures than in forgiveness.

"She had an affair of her own, you know."

"Was he at least a nice man?"

"Conrad, I'm not saying this to be cruel, but your mother didn't know any nice men."

"So they never forgave each other?"

My uncle Hector scratched his head and smiled. "Let's just say that in this family, forgiveness has a statute of limitations."

That made me laugh. "How long is the statute?"

Uncle Hector gave me a look. He had a sense of irony but he had no sense of humor. "If you're not on your knees within the week, it's over."

"Then why isn't anybody in this family divorced?"

"I don't have an answer for that."

I think my uncle Hector *did* have an answer for that. He just wasn't going to tell me. My own theory was that everybody in our family had the same phobia: they were all afraid of being happy.

Uncle Hector gently took the picture from my hands and stared at it. "It was taken in 1980, exactly one year and twelve days after your sister had been born. And it was taken at Martino's. I should know—I joined them for dinner that night. Your father was drunk, as you can see. And," he said as he pointed at the image of my mother, "Melissa was as untouchable and inscrutable as ever. She was always somewhere else—as if she was above being in the same room with anyone who resembled a human being. Just because she looked like an angel didn't mean she was one."

My uncle was a disappointed writer who read books "that didn't deserve to be published." He also had a penchant for dictionaries. It was a habit I picked up from him. He used to sit me on his lap when I was a boy and we would look up words. And he liked using all the words he looked up. Words like *inscrutable.* Not that his description of my mother was inaccurate. She was the most inscrutable woman who ever lived. She was a mystery no one ever solved. She admitted it herself. When I was eight, I was caught in the middle of an argument between her and my father. My father raged at her: "Who in the fuck are you, Melissa? *Just who the fuck are you?*"

My mother lit a cigarette and calmly whispered. "I am *un*knowable." She spoke the words slowly and with certainty. She blew out the smoke from her cigarette and added, "I thought that was why you married me, Octavio. And anyway, you don't like knowing women—you just like owning them."

My parents were theater. My sister Carmen and I were their audience. Even the photograph of the two of them that I am addicted to studying seems like a still from a movie.

My aunt Susan—who loved a man once but never married—said the photograph was taken at the Copacabana. "Loved that place. It opened up in 1979," she said. "Your parents went there a lot."

"Yes," she said, "it was definitely taken at the Copa. 1981. I remember the dress." My aunt Susan remembered dresses better than she remembered faces.

I didn't believe any of them. My uncles and aunts were the kind of people who liked to conceal more than they liked to reveal. I even took the photograph with me to Juárez one night and decided to venture into all the places that were still there. That was in 1999. I was seventeen and the violence hadn't erupted yet, and people still trafficked back and forth to have a drink and eat dinner. By 1999, the Hawaiian was long gone. I went into the Copa, studied the place and decided the picture had definitely not been taken there. I went to the Florida, a place that hadn't been mentioned but it definitely wasn't where the photograph had been taken either. I had a drink at the Kentucky Club and thought it was a possibility. I met my sister Carmen for dinner at Martino's that night and it was then that I decided that Martino's was the place. Definitely Martino's.

"You're probably right," Carmen said. "I hate that picture."

"Why?"

"Look at them, they're miserable."

"Yes, but they're beautiful too."

"You make a romance of them."

"*They were beautiful*," I repeated.

"Conrad, they were as fucked up as they were beautiful."

"I don't need to be reminded of things I already know." I smiled at her. We weren't fighting. Carmen and I didn't fight. "You have pictures of them too," I said.

"Yes," she said. "I have a picture of Dad with his shirt off, and he's smiling into the camera. And I have a picture of Mom looking straight into the camera as if she's daring the photographer to capture who she was. The camera lost the battle."

"I know those pictures," I said. "And it's Mom who told the truth about herself."

Carmen laughed. "I knew you were going to say something like that."

"I'm right. Dad's all smiles in the photograph. Looks aside, he didn't have anything inside him except anger and an insatiable sex drive. And Mom? She was Mom. She was exactly how she appears in the picture."

"Maybe you're right."

"Maybe?"

"Okay, so you're right. But being right about things doesn't mean a damn thing in this world."

She laughed and said, "Have you fallen in love yet?"

"I think I have," I said.

"Boy or girl?"

"Girl."

"Girl, really? I thought you'd settle for boys in the end."

"Well, I have time. And it's not as if I have to choose."

She smiled. "No. No, you don't, Conrad. So. Have you had sex?"

"Not yet," I said.

I wonder if she knew that I was lying to her.

"You know what I think? I think you're going to fall in love with sex. But I don't think you'll ever fall in love with a woman. With a man either. Sex. That's going to be your great love."

We both laughed. Carmen was five years older than I was, and we had more or less raised each other. She'd protected me all my life, held me when I was sad, told me the hard truths about whatever was happening in our strange and truth-evading family. Our parents never thought of us as children—and they certainly didn't treat us like children. They treated us like adults, spoke to us like adults. And they pretty much left us alone. I sometimes wonder if we didn't potty train ourselves. My father wasn't interested in being a father. And my mother wasn't interested in playing the role of nurturer.

I looked at Carmen sitting across from me. Beautiful Carmen. "And you?" I asked.

"Me? What?"

"Love. Any of that in your life?"

"Yes. I'm in love," she said.

"Really? When are you going to introduce me to him?"

"Tonight," she said.

I wondered why it mattered to me where that picture of my father and mother was taken. I think I wanted to know something factual about my parents. Most of what I knew about them was a lie—and even my own memories seemed unreliable to me. My mother suffered from depression and killed herself when I was ten. I didn't know what method she chose. I wasn't told the truth about the details of her death, but somehow the truth seeped into the air I breathed like a poison. My father killed a man with his bare fists in a drunken rage a couple of years later. He was killed while he was in prison. I'm certain he contributed to his own death with a rage he could never control.

Because my favorite hobby was listening to my uncles and aunts argue about nothing that really mattered, I brought up the competing versions of where that picture of my parents had been taken as often as I could. Once, during a boring Thanksgiving dinner, I simply said, "I was looking at the photograph. Uncle Hector says it was definitely taken at Martino's in 1980. I think I agree with him."

That got the conversation going. My aunt Lucille shook her head. "Oh, you and your photograph. I should never have given it to you."

My uncle Louie nodded, "Martino's or not, it *was* 1980."

"Perhaps," my aunt said.

My aunt Lucille wasn't Mexican. She was a woman from a humble background with pretentions—and she had a penchant for the word *perhaps*.

It annoyed my uncle who sometimes whispered to me that if I ever had any inclination to marry a gringa, I should go see a good therapist. "*Te hacen sufrir porque así son.* And don't ever believe anything your uncle Hector says about anything. He couldn't find his ass to take a dump."

I think I loved my two uncles and my aunts—I count Lucille here, an aunt by marriage only and a pain in the ass—because they provided comic relief. The fact that they didn't provide that service to me on purpose did nothing to diminish my gratitude. They could always make me smile and I had a great affection for them in my own superior way. They were a strange lot. They had a loyalty toward each other that was truly remarkable—especially when you took into account the fact that they didn't like each other very much. And even though they'd spent their lives on the border, they didn't behave like Mexicans. For reasons I didn't understand, they had abandoned their ethnic identities. There had been some money in the family, though I didn't know anything about that. In the part of the world that we lived in, they were an island unto themselves. They were disconnected from the culture around them. Their lives seemed something of a comedy to me—a sort of counterpoint to the tragic lives my parents had led.

I really didn't remember all that much about my mother and father. There were scenes of them that were stuck in my head but it didn't add up to a story. I remember my mother in a green satin dress and high heels as she was getting ready to go out one night. I must have been five. I remember her reaching down and placing her manicured fingers under my chin and whispering. "You'll be better looking than your father." She didn't say *I love you*. She didn't call me *amor*. She didn't tell me to be a good boy. She didn't tell me not to stay up too late. She didn't say *don't fight with your sister*. She didn't offer any words of love or advice. She didn't tell me what to do or not to do. She wasn't affectionate. She wasn't mean either—at least she wasn't mean to me. And she wasn't mean to Carmen either. She saved her meanness for my father. My mother handled us with a kindly and astounding indifference. I felt that she sometimes examined us with her eyes as if we were strange and foreign and even astonishing creatures. Most of the time, she lived in a dark, unreachable place, and even when she smiled or laughed, it always seemed to me that she didn't have it in her to be happy. Carmen once told me that our mother was a statue. "She could have been carved by Michelangelo." My sister hated my mother.

"She's not a statue," I said.

"I don't see why you defend her," she said. "She doesn't love you. She doesn't love anyone."

I didn't say anything. I knew she was right but I didn't want her to be right. I wanted my mother to love me.

I remember she didn't speak for weeks before she killed herself. I touched her and tried to make her see me. But she just stared blankly out into the room as if she was trying to find something that wasn't there. I took her hand. "Where does it hurt?" But it was as if I didn't exist and I knew she didn't hear my question.

My sister pulled me away. "It hurts everywhere," she said. "Can't you see that?"

I looked at Carmen and whispered, "I told you she wasn't a statue."

We weren't taken to my mother's funeral. My father descended into a permanent state of drunkenness. I don't remember how long it was after my mother died that my father took me in his arms and breathed me in. He kept smelling my neck. As I think back, I have the strangest idea that he was trying to find traces of my mother's smell somewhere in me. He held me and wept and I didn't know how to help him. My aunt Lucille gently pulled me away from him. My uncle Louie and my uncle Hector took me and Carmen to a movie. They always took us to movies. My uncle Louie said that even a bad movie could put you in a good mood.

To this day, I hate movies. They remind of me of my parents who disappeared. No movie has ever been made that could heal the wound of a boy who was born to parents who never loved him. It wasn't personal. My parents didn't love me because they couldn't. I didn't grow up feeling sorry for myself. I also didn't grow up lying to myself. I wasn't like anybody in my family. I never pretended I was someone I wasn't. I had no romantic versions of who and what I was. I saved that for Carmen. I think I also saved all my love for her without even knowing why. Maybe I *did* know something of the why. I loved her honesty and I loved her kindness. She raised me without pretending to be my mother. And she never resented my presence.

She would read entire books to me, one chapter at a time. They weren't literary books. They were books like *Valley of the Dolls*—Jacqueline Susann and Harold Robbins schlock. I loved her voice when she read to me and I got lost in the world of cheesy novels where the characters behaved more or less like my parents had behaved.

When Carmen turned eighteen, she told my uncle Louie and my aunt Lucille—who raised her after my mother killed herself—that she was leaving.

"But where will you go?"

"I have a job," she said. "And I'm going to school."

"You'll starve out there," my uncle Louie said. "What's wrong with you?"

Carmen kissed my uncle on the cheek, looked straight into my aunt Lucille's eyes, then looked back at my uncle Louie. "You really should leave her, you know." She smiled and walked out the door.

Lucille was rendered speechless. After Carmen left, she looked at my uncle and said, "I'll never let her back into this house."

My uncle shrugged. "You really think she'll ever want to come back?"

My aunt Lucille, wearing her customary frigid expression, shook her head and said, "She's just like her mother."

My aunt, who was wrong about most things, wasn't wrong about that one thing. At least she wasn't all wrong. I realized by then that my mother had been mentally ill. And I had a feeling that Carmen was moving in the same direction. But while my mother had been distant and sad, Carmen was kindhearted and affectionate. I think her mental illness was far worse than my mother's.

That night, when I was seventeen and after we'd eaten dinner at Martino's, Carmen *did* introduce me to the man she was in love with. Only it wasn't a man. It wasn't a woman either. Marijuana. It was the first time I got high.

She lived in an old apartment building near downtown. My uncle Hector owned it. He didn't charge her rent. My uncle Louie and my aunt Lucille didn't know anything about their arrangement. They had broken all ties with Carmen, not that Carmen cared. Uncle Hector had given her some of my mother's furniture that he'd kept in a storage unit. They were antiques. And at least Uncle Hector wasn't a slum lord. He was obsessed with history and part of that obsession was restoring old buildings.

Entering Carmen's apartment, with its high ceilings and wood floors, was like entering another era. She'd even acquired an old Victrola and liked to play Billie Holiday records—my mother's favorite singer. She had black and white photographs on the walls. It might have been 1940.

When we got to her apartment that night, she poured me a glass of wine and took out her stash. She rolled a joint and taught me how to roll one too. I was a quick study. I loved the high. I'd never been that relaxed in my life and it seemed that the possibility of happiness actually existed. We laughed. We talked.

I confessed to her that I'd already had sex. "Sorry I lied," I said.

"I knew you were lying."

"How? I'm a pretty good liar."

"You are. It runs in the family. But you can't lie to me. You just can't." She smiled, then laughed.

I laughed too. "Carmen, maybe it's because I don't *want* to lie to you. It's nice, to tell the truth."

She leaned over and kissed me on the cheek. "Don't ever leave me," she said.

"Not ever," I said.

"So tell me about the girl you slept with."

"She's in college."

"How'd you meet?"

"Starbucks. Her name is Serena."

"Serena? That's sweet. How was the sex?"

I pointed my joint in her direction. "It was fucking great. Much better than this shit."

"So, are you in love?"

"I might be."

"You're seventeen."

"Seventeen? Shit. Seventeen in our family? That means I'm at least thirty."

Carmen just looked at me and shrugged.

"We were taught to speak like adults who'd been to college when we were six. Kids used to make fun of me in middle school because I talked like a fucking English teacher. Fucking seventeen, Carmen? We're old. We were never young, not ever." My voice was cracking. I was crying. I'd been happy with that first hit, and now I was crying.

"Don't cry, Conrad. Don't look back." She smiled. "Take another hit."

I did. And I leaned back and looked up at the ceiling. "I like this stuff," I said.

"Me too." She just smiled at me. "You know what I think? I think you're in love with the sex."

"Is that so bad?"

"I don't know." I loved her smile. I knew she wasn't a happy person, but when she smiled I almost believed she'd have a good life. "You know, Conrad, maybe it's better to love sex without having to love the person you're having sex with. It's less complicated."

"I'm not sure what to think about that," I said.

"My problem, Conrad, is that I fall in love. I always wind up falling in love. It hurts. I've decided against it."

"Is it something you can decide?"

"There's a lot of things you can decide. Me, I've decided to try every drug in the universe."

That scared me. That really scared me. I knew she meant it. "Why?"

"I'm sad, Conrad."

"I know."

"I get depressed."

"Have you seen someone?"

"I went to a therapist for awhile. She told me what I already knew. That I suffer from depression. She gave me pills."

"Do you take them?"

"Sometimes."

She took a drag from her joint. She smiled. "What's wrong with a little happiness?"

Carmen was right. I was more in love with sex than with the people I slept with. I had sex with Serena for about six months. But then it got old with her. I wanted that high again. I broke up with her. She didn't seem to mind all that much. She kissed me on the cheek and said, "It was fun, the sex part, anyway." She looked at me. "Conrad, I like you. But you want to hear the truth?"

The truth? What the hell. I could always use a little of that. "Sure," I said.

"You're not a lot of fun, Conrad. You're four years younger than me—"

I interrupted her. "And already I act like an old man."

She nodded. "Well, not an old man, exactly—but serious, not, well, you know, you don't know how to have fun."

"The sex was fun," I said. I felt like an idiot even as I said it.

"And that was about as far as it went."

"So how come you just didn't, I mean, why didn't you just come out and say it?"

"You're strange, different. You're sophisticated and smart and articulate. But you're aloof. I like you, Conrad. There's something about you that's real."

Then she laughed. "And, in case you hadn't noticed, you're beautiful to look at."

I thought of what Carmen had said about my mother. *She's a statue.*

I slept with another girl a week later. God, we did everything that night. She wasn't really a girl. She was a woman, much older than me. She had some real experience behind her and I learned more than a few tricks that night. Not that I hadn't imagined doing them. I also discovered one other thing: it was easy for me to get picked up, and I knew why. I remember what my mother told me as boy, *You'll be much better looking than your father.* I was. I didn't mistake my looks for virtue. But my face was going to be my co-conspirator in my obsession with sex. Or maybe it wasn't an obsession. I had just turned eighteen. Maybe I was just normal. But normal didn't really run in our family.

I thought of Carmen, how she said she was going to experiment with every mood-altering substance in existence. Maybe I was just like her. Only my drug of choice was sex. Sex was all I thought of after that night in the hotel with a woman whose name I had already forgotten.

I decided to stay home and go to college. I didn't have money and a degree was a degree. And I had always liked living on the border. Unlike my uncles and aunts, I liked hearing all the Spanish and liked speaking it—even if I mangled half the words. I couldn't see myself living anywhere else. Maybe it had something to do with my mother and my father—I don't know. I sometimes analyzed myself—but I didn't take it very far. It was Carmen who was the therapist in the family.

I didn't know what I was going to study. English probably, because of my obsession with language. Well, it wasn't exactly an obsession. I was good at writing and terrible at math. So the decision was practical. And anyway, I wasn't very ambitious. Who the hell knew what I was going to become? In the meantime, I had a new girlfriend. There weren't girls at the high school I was graduating from because it was a Catholic school for boys. My aunt Lucille had insisted. "We're sending you to Cathedral High and that's the end of it." I didn't have any say in the matter. But one day after school I walked to the university and struck up a conversation with a girl named Liz. We started having sex a week later. I think she enjoyed the sex more than I did. We couldn't keep our hands off each other. After graduation, we saw more and more of each other. The sex got less exciting, but I really liked her. I thought maybe I could even fall in love with her. Why not? Except that I cheated on her.

I informed Uncle Louie about my decision to attend the University of Texas at El Paso. He didn't really say much. I was on my way out the door to spend the weekend at my sister's apartment. She'd called me on my cell and told me, "I scored some good shit, and Antonio's out of my life." So I was off for a weekend of partying with my sister.

When I got to her place, she said, "Okay, I'm going to bitch for five minutes and then I'm done, okay? Did you know Uncle Hector paid for my college? Did you know that?"

"No. You never told me that."

She looked at me. "Are you mad?"

"No. But, well, we're supposed to tell each other the truth. I thought that's how we played it."

"Don't be mad."

"You said you got loans." I smiled. "I'm not mad. Why didn't you just come out and tell me? What's the big deal?"

"Because I'm ashamed of myself."

"Why?"

"Because I hate my fucking job. Uncle Hector bribed me."

"Bribed you?"

"He made a deal with me. If I went to college and got a major in something practical, then he'd pay for all of my expenses. I mean already I live rent free. I didn't know what to do and, well, here I am a fucking CPA."

"I thought it was because you were good at math."

"Yeah, well, I am. I don't know how I made it through college. I was—I don't want to talk about it. The thing is that I hate my fucking job. Look, Conrad, don't make the same mistake I made. If Uncle Hector wants to make a deal with you, tell him to shove his money up his ass."

I smiled. "So far I've had no offers."

She laughed.

"Quit," I said. "Do something else. The arts. You'd be good at that."

She laughed.

"You would be," I said. "I'm serious."

I followed her into the kitchen where she opened a bottle of wine. She poured us both a glass. "Tonight, something special." She had this look in her eyes. She took a couple of small plastic baggies out of her purse. I knew what it was right away. "A little something to brighten up your otherwise boring existence in Aunt Lucille's spotless house."

I didn't say anything. I just watched her put the powder on a plate. She divided it into straight little lines with a credit card. I studied her as she intently took out a twenty dollar bill and rolled it up tightly. Presto, it was a small straw. She snorted a line of coke up her nose in an instant. Then she did another line. She handed me the rolled-up bill. I didn't really want to do this shit. But I was powerless in her presence. So I just went along for the ride. It wasn't going to kill me.

I have to say that it was great. I'd never felt anything like I was feeling right then. But this was the thought that passed through my head: *I wonder what it would be like to have sex while I was on this shit.*

Saturday morning, Carmen and I slept in. Then we went to a movie. She knew I hated them. But she'd bought my uncles' theory on movies making you happy. I stood in line to buy popcorn and Carmen disappeared into the women's bathroom. I knew what she was up to. A moment of panic shot through me. I knew that drugs for Carmen were not simply recreational. Maybe she wasn't an addict yet, but she would be. And I knew there was nothing I could do about it.

On Saturday night, Carmen brought out the coke again. I got high with her. She wanted to do more. She said, "Let's walk over to the bars."

"The bars?"

"The gay bars down the street. I know someone who can hook us up for more."

Us, I thought? *Us?* I took a sip from my glass of wine. "I'm not twenty-one," I said. I didn't want to do any more shit.

"Oh, you can just hang around outside. All the smokers, they hang around on the sidewalk. You can just hang there until I take care of business."

Even the way she was talking was changing.

"Sure," I said. I could never say no.

She smiled as we walked out the door. "Besides, you just might get lucky and get picked up by some hunk."

The thought hadn't crossed my mind. But I hung on to that thought. I'd thought about being with guys—and maybe this was my chance.

It wasn't a long walk to the bars. Carmen was happy and high. She asked about our uncles and aunts. "I only see Uncle Hector," she said. "And even then, not very often. The others don't contact me. They're too afraid of Lucille to cross her." She laughed. "What a fucked-up family."

"Well," I said. "They're more boring than fucked up."

"How much do you know about them?"

I shrugged. "Nothing really. I mean they raised us. That's what I know."

"Oh," she said. "I have stories." By then we'd reached the strip of bars on Stanton Street—and the bars were hopping. There was this look of euphoria on her face. She walked into one of the bars, a place called the Toolbox. Subtle. "Just hang out. This won't take long."

I felt a little uncomfortable. I leaned against the wall and watched the scene. A guy came up to me. I guessed he was in his late twenties. He had dark eyes, thick wavy hair and a nice smile. He wore a tight T-shirt and it was obvious that he went to the gym. "Hi," he said.

"Hi," I said.

"Can I buy you a drink?"

"Not old enough," I said. I was always good at hiding my nervousness.

"You don't need an ID in my apartment."

I was definitely interested. "Can't tonight. I'm with someone."

"I'm with someone too," he said.

"My sister. I'm just waiting for her." I took my cell out of my pocket. I handed it to him. "Name and number," I said.

He smiled, took my cell phone and punched in his name and number. He handed my cell phone back to me. "Mark," he said.

"Conrad," I said.

"Call," he said as he walked into the bar.

"I promise," I said.

My sister stepped out into the street and we walked back to her place.

She did more lines of coke, but I didn't. I was tired. I stayed up with her. "C'mon," she urged me, "just one more line."

She had some tequila on the table. I poured myself a shot and downed it. "That's it for me. I'm going to bed."

As I was lying in the dark, I thought of the road my sister was taking. And then I thought of Mark. That was the road I was going to take.

On Sunday afternoon, I was back at my aunt's place. That was where I'd lived since my mother had "died." Not that it had ever felt like home. It was my aunt Lucille's home. Hers and hers alone. Even my uncle Louie was a visitor there. After having spent the weekend with Carmen, it was a relief to be in an environment that didn't have dark and dangerous corners. Carmen had driven me home—but I knew she wasn't going back to her place. She was all dressed up and I knew she was going out. I also knew what she was looking for.

My uncles and aunts were gathered in the living room, having their traditional Sunday afternoon happy hour. The smell of my aunt Lucille's roast permeated the house. The smell of her cooking gave me a sense of comfort. What I didn't know was that they were all gathered to intervene. That's exactly what it was—an intervention.

My aunt Lucille took the lead. "I understand you're going to this university in the fall." I almost laughed at the disdain in the *this university*.

"Yes," I said. "I didn't apply anywhere else."

"With your grades, you could have gotten in anywhere."

"And with my money, where would I have gotten in?"

"You should have asked us. You should have consulted with us."

"What's wrong with going to school here?"

"You're better than that. You're smarter than that."

My aunt Susan, who was as quiet as she was lovely, put up her hand and motioned for my aunt Lucille to stop. "Don't you want to experience anything else but this nothing of a town?"

"I don't feel that way about this town," I said. "I like it here. I like the border. I like the people."

"And you don't want to leave your sister," Uncle Louie added.

"No, I don't."

"She'll hold you back," Lucille said.

"Hold me back from what? Haven't you noticed I'm not exactly the most ambitious young man on the planet?"

"You're smart, smart, smart," Uncle Hector said. "Don't underestimate yourself."

I wasn't going to win this argument with them. I wanted to ask for a drink, but that wasn't going to happen. "It's too late anyway. School starts in six weeks."

"Well, next year you're transferring to a better school like U.T. Austin. Getting you out of this town will do you a world of good—and that's that." Aunt Lucille was adamant. "We'll all take care of the money. That's not an issue."

I wanted to say, "Doesn't it matter what I want?" But I didn't. Lucille controlled the family. Control is how she loved. But it was true what they said. I couldn't bear to leave Carmen. I knew her life was going to hell, and even if I couldn't keep her from going there, I was willing to go to hell with her.

I sat there quietly, my uncles' and aunts' eyes on me. "I know you love me," I said. And it was true, they did love me. But their love was material and contained little or no affection. I don't know why, but tears were rolling down my face. I wiped them away. "I'm hungry," I said.

Uncle Louie put his hand on my shoulder. "Let's eat then."

Uncle Hector had bought an apartment complex not far from the university and let me have one of the apartments there. Rent free, of course. It wasn't in Carmen's neighborhood. He made sure of that. But it wasn't far either. "You need to have your own place," he said. "I think Lucille's right that you should try to maintain a distance from your sister. But in my opinion, you also need to get away from Lucille." He tossed me a set of keys—one was to my new apartment, the other was to the new car he'd bought for me.

"So do you ever see Carmen?" I asked.

"I used to stop by and see her. I don't anymore."

I studied his face.

"Don't ask me why, Conrad. I think you already know."

My aunt Lucille and my uncle Louie took me shopping for furniture. A bed, kitchen utensils, pots, pans, sheets, towels, a dresser, curtains, coffee table, book shelves. Kitchen table and chairs, couch, reading chair and a new laptop computer. They, of course, chose everything for me. They never asked if I liked their choices. But then again, I didn't really care. I smiled a lot, made small talk, behaved exactly like they had taught me to behave and the whole shopping-for-my-apartment thing was relatively painless. And what the hell, it wasn't my money. My aunt Lucille cooked the first meal in my new place. I was allowed a glass of wine with dinner. The talk centered around the good grades I was going to get so that I could immediately transfer to Austin. "It's such a nice town," Aunt Susan said. "I'm sure you'll find a beautiful girl there."

I smiled. But I wasn't smiling at what she said. I was smiling at what I was thinking: *There's lots of beautiful girls here too. And lots of beautiful boys.*

The first night in my apartment, I called Mark.

"It's Conrad," I said. "Remember me?"

"I remember," he said. "How could I forget?"

"I've never been with a guy," I said. "Willing to teach me?"

It took him twenty minutes to arrive at my place. He had his tongue down my throat the minute he walked through the door. He undressed me. I undressed him.

Sleeping with men became my new addiction. But I would go back to women sometimes. The problem was that women expected more. Men felt no remorse about one-night stands.

I visited Carmen two or three times a week. She'd lost a little weight. She looked tired to me—but if you didn't know her, you wouldn't be able to tell. She knew how to wear makeup and she was a beautiful, beautiful woman. I knew she was doing all kinds of shit. "You're not taking your meds, are you?"

"Don't judge, Conrad."

"I'm not judging. You know me better. I just worry."

She kissed me on the cheek. "You're sweet."

"Don't be condescending," I said. She kissed me on the cheek again. "I'm not being condescending. I adore you."

"I adore you too," I said.

"Conrad, I'm not always depressed, you know? Look at me. Don't I look good?"

"Beautiful," I said.

"You worry too much."

I knew she went up and down. Right now she was up. When she was down, she didn't call me. It had always been that way. When she was in high school, she'd spend hours, days, weeks in her room. And then she was fine again. I knew how it was with her. She didn't particularly like talking about her mood swings. And she wasn't going to listen to anything I had to say about that subject.

"How's your sex life?" she asked. She was smirking. "Do you go a week without having sex with someone?"

I shrugged.

"Can you go two days without having sex with someone?"

I wanted to ask her if she could go just one day without ingesting a mood-altering substance. It was true, I was afraid for her. But what I was really afraid of was losing her.

College was fine. I studied. I was a good student and found my classes mildly interesting. I was particularly interested in two of my professors. One of them was a young professor who taught political science. She had thick brown hair and beautiful blue eyes. She didn't try to be sexy or any of that. But I daydreamed of what it would be like to undress her. The other was a history professor, a man in his late thirties. He was handsome in a very intellectual way. He had dark eyes and wore very hip designer glasses. He sometimes didn't shave for a few days and it made him look like he might be the kind of guy who liked to flirt with danger. He didn't wear a wedding ring. There were two hundred students in his lecture class. I sat near the front of the class and made a list of the things I would have liked to do with him in bed.

When I started school, I had applied for a student loan. I didn't need it but I lied on the application. Well, it wasn't exactly a lie. My parents *were* deceased and I was on my own. I said nothing about my uncles and aunts and their income. Who would know? My uncles and aunts put money directly into my account. That money was to pay for my tuition and to live on. They were generous. I was their communal property. They had money and nothing much to spend it on. They didn't want me to work. They wanted me to be a good student so I could move to Austin and make something of myself. I qualified for work study, worked twenty hours a week and put all the money away. There was a reason for this. I thought Carmen might be in trouble. I knew she was getting in deeper and deeper. I had this bad feeling. What if she needed my help? What was she going to do? Who would she turn to?

I saved as much money as I could. Just in case.

One night, I was lying in bed with a guy I'd met. His name was Rick and I liked him. We were actually having a conversation. I was wondering if maybe this would turn into something more than sex. My cell phone rang. It was Carmen. "I need you."

"Where are you?"

"I need to go home. I need to get home." She was upset, and her voice was cracking and she sounded scared. "You have to come for me."

"Where are you?"

"The Mesa Inn."

"What room?"

She was standing outside her hotel room. I got out of the car and she fell into my arms. I held her. "Let's get you home," I said. She cried all the way back.

When we got to her place, I gave her some hot tea. I put a blanket around her. She was trembling. I wasn't going anywhere. I was going to get the story whether she wanted to tell me or not.

We sat in the quiet of the room, not saying anything. Finally, her tears and trembling stopped and a kind of calmness washed over her. "Music?" she whispered, then smiled.

I put on Billie Holiday, then changed my mind and put on Kurt Elling, her favorite jazz singer. I sat on the couch across from her as she sank into her leather chair. "I'd like a drink," she said. I poured us both a glass of wine. I put hers on the coffee table, then leaned over and kissed her forehead.

I sat down. "Talk," I said.

She reached for her wine. "I'm tired," she said.

"So am I. So talk today or talk tomorrow. I'm not going anywhere. Think I'll spend the night."

"What? Afraid I'll sneak out again?"

"No, you don't have wheels. Where's your car?"

"He took it."

"He?"

"He tried to rape me."

"He?"

"Okay," she said. "There's this guy. His name's Freddy. Nice-looking guy. He's a dealer. But he's a user too. He scored some ice."

"Ice?"

"Crystal meth."

"I'm listening."

She smiled at me. "You know, you just might make a good therapist."

I smiled back. "I'd rather pass a kidney stone."

She laughed. She seemed so herself at that moment. "What the fuck do you know about kidney stones?"

"I had to take Uncle Louie to the hospital when he had them. He was writhing on the floor of the car as I drove to the emergency room."

"I think I would have liked to witness that."

"Don't be mean." We both smiled at each other.

"So this sonofabitch Freddy. Well, we smoked. He taught me how to—"

"Don't need the details."

"Yeah, well, we got high. God, what a high. Euphoria. Like nothing I've ever experienced. So Freddy gets horny on this shit. Not that I wasn't. But Freddy's not for me. So he tries to rip off my clothes. And I push him away. But it doesn't matter. So I grab my keys and he's trying to keep me from opening the door. Lucky for me that Freddy's five-six and weighs not too much over a hundred pounds. I belt him and I walk out into the parking lot. But I'm high, and even though I was a little scared, I still felt great. So Freddy follows me out, grabs my keys and takes off in my car. I don't know what to do, but that stuff, I mean I felt like I could do anything, like I wanted to walk, just walk. So that's what I did. And I was singing and I thought of calling Antonio and telling him to come over and maybe we could patch things up between us—and then I remembered my cell phone was in the hotel room and I didn't have the key. But the room was in my name so I just went up to the desk and I got another key and walked back into the room. My cell phone was still there. So I was there, in the room, alone, just high. I called Antonio. He came by. We had sex. It was great. The high lasts so long." She pulled her hair back. "But then, eventually, I came down. Antonio left. And I don't know why, but all of a sudden, I found myself crying and shaking, and I don't know, Conrad, I don't know what I'm doing."

I didn't know what to say. Finally I just said, "What's Freddy's number?"

"What are you going to do?"

"What's his number?"

She handed me her cell phone. I used mine instead of hers to call him. I knew he probably had her name in his phone and would refuse to answer. I heard his voice, "Yeah? You looking for something?" I took it he was used to getting phone calls from referrals.

"I'll tell you what. If you don't return my sister's car to the Mesa Inn, I'm gonna call the fuckin' cops. You got that, Freddy? If you don't, your ass is gonna be in the fucking can. Twenty minutes, Mesa Inn." I hung up the phone.

"Trying to be my hero?"

I nodded. "Something like that."

"Let's go," I said.

She didn't say a word on the way back to the Mesa Inn. But finally, she said, "What makes you think he'll be there?"

"Because he's not gonna take the chance. And you know what, I *will* call the cops if he's not there. I fucking will, Carmen."

"What will you tell them?"

"I haven't thought that far ahead."

"You should be afraid of guys like him, Conrad."

"So should you," I said. "And besides, he's five-six and a little over a hundred pounds. Isn't that what you said?"

She nodded.

"I'm six-one and a hundred-and-eighty-five pounds."

When I pulled into the parking lot, I saw Carmen's car. No one was in it. I opened the door and the keys were on the seat along with Carmen's purse and a note that said, *Bitch, you better keep away.*

I walked back to my car. "Can you drive?"

She nodded.

I drove her car back to her place. She drove mine.

I handed her the note when we were back in her apartment. "Carmen," I said. "Doesn't that scare you?"

"No," she said.

"Well, it fucking scares me."

"Scared? You didn't look too scared when you were on the phone with Freddy."

"Carmen, you don't get it. I'm not scared for me. I'm scared for you." I'm not much of a crier, but I was crying. I was sobbing actually. I felt her arms around me. "Shhh, baby," she said. "Shhh."

I woke up at noon and found myself lying on Carmen's couch. I walked into the kitchen and put on a pot of coffee. I heard the water running. Carmen was in the shower. I stared at the coffee dripping into the glass coffeepot. A scene ran through my head, my father sitting in the kitchen, pouring vodka into his coffee. He was pressing his finger to his lips and smiling at me, *shhhhh*. Scenes in my head and yet no real story. I realized I didn't know if I loved or hated my father. It was as if he existed to be watched, but *not* to be known, *not* to be understood.

I poured myself a cup of coffee and walked back into the living room. Carmen was sitting in her leather chair, her long dark hair still wet. Even in her robe, she looked like she was dressed to go out. She had a fragile elegance. I smiled at her. "Coffee?"

She nodded.

"Still take three spoons of sugar?"

"There's enough bitterness in my life, don't you think? I like it sweet."

I shook my head. When I walked back into the kitchen and scooped three spoons of sugar into her cup of coffee, I saw the needle on the shelf. I stood there for a moment. I put the coffee cup down and picked up the needle and examined it. I don't know why. I knew what it was for. She'd talked about heroin before but I thought she'd never really try it. Maybe I was becoming like my uncles and aunts, refusing to look at what was happening around me. And I thought I was so fucking honest about things. I walked back into the living room and handed Carmen her cup of coffee.

"We won't live to be old," she said. "We're like Mom and Dad."

"No, we're not," I said.

She looked at me. She had my mother's piercing green eyes. "Did you know that you can't walk down a street without someone turning back to look at you?"

"What?"

"You're beautiful, Conrad. Handsome. People look at you. They want to keep looking at you."

"What's your point?"

"Me too, Conrad. I walk into a bar or a restaurant and I get looks."

"Is there a point to this conversation, Carmen?"

"We're like our parents."

"Because we have fucking good genes? I don't get where you're going here, Carmen."

"You sound angry."

"Maybe. Maybe I'm just frustrated."

"Conrad, beauty is a fucking curse. You can look at any woman, any man, and, if you want, you can take them home. They'll worship your body for a night. You'll worship theirs. It's euphoric, isn't it?"

"Yes," I whispered.

"Always chasing the dragon?"

"What?"

"Chasing the dragon, Conrad. You know the expression?"

"No."

She pulled her hair back over her ears. "When you get a high. That first hit, that first fantastic, euphoric hit. It's the dragon." The smile on her face, the clenched fist, almost crazed and yet that look was almost beatific, almost as if she'd seen the face of God. "You catch the dragon. And the rest of the night, you spend trying to catch the fucking dragon again. And sometimes you do," she said. "Sometimes you do." She sipped on her coffee. "That's you, Conrad. That moment of climax, that fucking climax, those few seconds when you've had a taste of the apocalypse in the touch of another man or another woman. You want to do it again and again. And the dragon reappears. And after a while, he disappears and you go looking for him again. And you find another body. And you find him again, the dragon, and you want to live with him forever. But you can't."

I didn't want to hear it. I didn't want to hear any of it. I didn't care how hard and how cruel and how true her words were. I didn't want the pursuits of my life put into words. I didn't. I almost hated her at that moment—except that I could never hate her. She was the only real thing in my life—Carmen, and the dragon I was chasing.

We sat and drank our coffee in silence. I felt so old. I felt as if I had always been old. Even when I was a boy sitting on Uncle Hector's lap, him explaining words and concepts that were beyond me. Somehow, they weren't beyond me. I was born old. I had never been a boy. I had never spoken like a boy. I had never acted like a boy. I had never thought like a boy. I looked up at Carmen and I knew I was wearing a tired look that was begging her to stay quiet and not start talking again. But she wasn't going to.

"Conrad, we're all chasing the dragon. Me and drugs. I can't stop. I tell myself I'll stop. And I can't. And a part of me never wants to stop. It takes away the sadness, and it makes things better—and it makes them worse. I can't stop. I live for the dragon."

"You can stop," I said. "I'll help you."

"Can you stop, Conrad?"

"Yes. I can stop."

"Really?"

"Yes."

"How many men have you slept with? How many women? Can you still count them?"

"Yes."

"You still know their names?"

"Yes. Carmen, why are you doing this?"

"And next year, Conrad, will you be able to count them? Will you be able to remember their names? Mom and Dad, I don't think they had much of a conscience. But we do, Conrad. So we're fucked. But in some ways *we are* just like them. They had a different dragon. They had this passion for each other. This beautiful, destructive, explosive passion that made them intensely alive. They were more alive in their short lives than any of our pathetic uncles and aunts. Mom and Dad, they couldn't leave each other. There was that dragon they were chasing. The dragon was inside of each of them and they knew it and they wanted to live there forever. The dragon lived in Mother's eyes and Dad's rage and they couldn't stop. They just couldn't stop. And Lucille? Her dragon? Control. It makes her high as a kite. That moment when she knows she controls everyone in the room—that's when she catches her dragon. And Susan. Broken, broken Susan. She ran away to Mexico with some man she didn't even know. She came back five years later and she was nothing more than a fucking shadow. She caught her dragon—and the dragon almost killed her. But at least she had a taste of it. Not like Uncle Hector. Gay. Gay, gay, gay. He never had the courage to chase the dragon. But at least he knew the dragon was there to be chased. Uncle Louie? And Uncle Louie, poor bastard. If I explained the dragon to him, he'd look at me like I was insane. Poor, poor Uncle Louie. No imagination. No dragons for him. I'd rather be dead."

"Stop," I said.

"Why?" she said. "I'm telling you the truth."

"That's why I want you to stop."

I began to throw myself into my studies. I wanted to forget about my dragon. I started smoking. I liked the idea of it. I liked the feel of the smoke when I blew it out through my nose. I felt sophisticated, like I was in one of those old movies my uncle Louie liked so much.

I called Carmen every day. I wanted to hear her voice. I wanted to reassure myself that everything was going to be okay. More often than not, I got her voicemail. Sometimes she returned my phone calls, sometimes she didn't. When I texted her, she texted me back. I thought she was avoiding me. Sometimes I'd stop by in the evening and she wasn't there. One night we had dinner. She cooked. Somehow that made me feel better, made me feel that our lives, hers and mine, were normal. When we sat down to eat she said, "We won't talk about the dragon."

"Good," I said. But I studied her that night. She had acquired my mother's ethereal gaze. It was as if she was looking at something that I couldn't see. And yet, when she pointed her piercing eyes in my direction, there was a tenderness there that almost made me want to cry. I had never thought of myself as a sentimental man. And I wasn't. I was anything *but* sentimental. I was aloof. And I was often superior. But not when it came to Carmen. My love for her was a kind of insanity. I wanted to hold onto her forever. And yet I knew I *couldn't* hold onto her. She too was a kind of dragon. A dragon I would never catch. A dragon that would forever evade me.

I went a week without having sex. A week became two weeks, then three, then four. But all I could think about was catching the dragon. Then one Thursday night, at one o'clock in the morning, I just couldn't stand it. I walked to the bars. I stood out on the sidewalk and smoked a cigarette. I decided to go into one of the bars. Maybe they wouldn't card me. I looked like a man. Certainly I looked like I could be twenty-one. I ordered a drink. I got served. I finished my drink. I ordered another. The bar would be closing soon. A guy came up to me. "Never seen you in here before."

"I don't get out much," I said.

He was handsome. He took me home with him. That night, I caught the dragon. I thought of what Carmen had said, *that one moment when you've had a taste of the apocalypse.* I walked home the next morning. He didn't live far. When I put my key into the door, I realized I didn't even remember his name. I found myself crying in the shower. I called Carmen. She didn't answer. I texted her. She didn't answer. I called her at work. I got her voicemail. I decided to call the main number to her work. The secretary said she'd been out all week with the flu. I went to class. I texted her all day. I went to her apartment. She didn't answer the doorbell. Her car wasn't there.

I had this feeling. I had this awful feeling.

I went home. I smoked cigarette after cigarette. I had a friend from school, not a good friend—I didn't have good friends. But he was as close as I got. He was twenty-three. After dropping out of college, he returned to El Paso. He said he wanted something better for himself. I liked him. He was nice looking, very straight, a good boy. His name was Adam and he was in my history class. I called him. I asked him if he'd buy some liquor for me. "You're not twenty-one? You seem older."

"I get that a lot."

"No, I don't mean that you look older. I mean you act older."

"I'm not boyish if that's what you mean."

He laughed. "Yeah, I guess that's what I mean."

I met him at the liquor store. He bought me some bourbon and some gin. The good stuff. "If you're going to drink, then have some class."

He came over. I wanted to tell him about my sister. But I couldn't. We had a drink and talked. It was a relief to have someone in the room with me, something other than the panic that loomed over me and the rooms of my apartment. Adam looked around and searched the place with his eyes. "Wow," he said. "A real adult lives here."

"That doesn't sound like a compliment."

"You're eighteen years old. You have furniture. Everything is in its place. I have an eighteen-year-old brother who doesn't know how to button his fucking shirt. And look at this place. Artsy black and white photographs on the wall, a real painting, books on the shelf—and I bet you've read most of them."

"The photographs and the painting are courtesy of my sister. And the books are there for show."

"Sure," he said.

There was a picture of her and me on top of my bookcase. He pointed at the picture. "Is that her?"

"Yeah."

"How old is she?"

"Carmen's about to turn twenty-four."

"Does she have a boyfriend?"

We smiled at each other.

"Not right now." I laughed. "But I'm her brother, not her pimp."

He laughed. "Sorry. I'm an idiot."

"No," I said, "you're not. You're just a guy." And he was just a guy, a nice guy. I wondered if my sister liked nice guys. I had a funny feeling she didn't. I think she liked danger. I think we both did.

Adam looked at his watch. He downed his drink. "We should hang out sometime," he said. "Right now I have a date."

I smiled at him. "Boy or girl?"

"Girl." He didn't seem at all bothered by my question. He looked at me. "So you like boys?"

"Girls too," I said. "My sister says I just like sex."

"You're eighteen. You're supposed to like sex. Playing for both teams increases your chances considerably." He shrugged. "Liking sex. That makes you pretty fucking normal, don't you think?" I liked that he thought that. But normal was something I would never be.

When he left, the thought crossed my mind that it would be nice if I started making friends with people. Friends. Real friends. Everybody didn't have to be a potential lover. *Life didn't have to be like this.*

I envied Adam. He would marry a pretty girl and love her and have kids. And they would have everyday problems and have good and decent lives because they were good and decent people. I didn't think of myself as being decent. What was I? What the fuck was I? I tried texting Carmen again.

Answer. Answer. I watched television and drank gin and tonics. I turned off the television when I realized that I didn't even know what show I was watching. I looked at the time on my cell. It was one o'clock. I went to bed but couldn't sleep. I got up and downed another gin and tonic. I went back to bed. I dozed off, but jumped up when I heard my cell phone ring. It was Carmen.

"Where are you?" I said.

She sounded tired and stoned out of her mind. "Come," she said.

"Where are you?"

"I'm at the Budget Hotel."

"The Budget Hotel?" I was running hotels through my head. And then it came to me. "That hotel behind Lucy's on Mesa?"

"Yes," she whispered.

She'd left the door to her room ajar. I walked in. She was sitting on the floor, and the lamp in the room cast a shadow on her face. There was a needle next to her. She smiled at me. "Sweetheart," she whispered. "I caught the dragon." She handed me the needle. "It's ready for you," she said.

I didn't say anything.

"Take it," she said.

I took the needle away from her.

"Do it," she said.

I stood there frozen.

She smiled and whispered my name. "Conrad. Conrad. Die with me."

Her look, that look—I panicked. "What did you do? What did you do?" I took her and held her in my arms. And I knew she was slipping. She started convulsing and I remember yelling, *No! No!* I don't remember calling 911 but I must have—because the ambulance came. I was rocking her in my arms.

They took her away and I just stood there in a stupor. The cops took me with them to the emergency room. The hospital wasn't far and they were gentle with me.

I whispered her name, *Carmen*, as if by whispering her name I could bring her back. But she was gone.

I remember talking to the police as I stood in the emergency waiting room. I don't remember what I said. One of the officers was very kind. "Is there anyone we should call?"

I nodded. I gave him my cell. "Uncle Hector," I said.

None of it seemed real. I kept thinking, *No, no, this isn't happening*. I was sitting there, just sitting. I made myself perfectly still. I'd become my mother, the statue. My uncle Hector and my uncle Louie appeared in front of me. They tried to comfort me but I was inconsolable. "I want to see her," I said.

"Are you sure?"

I nodded.

They let us see her. She was lying on the bed, a sheet over her face. I uncovered her. They'd closed her eyes. I would never see them again. I found myself yelling, *Goddamn you! Goddamn you! You left me! You fucking left me! You and Mom, you just left me!*

It would be a lie to say that I remembered her funeral. The day we buried her, I went to her apartment. I asked Uncle Hector for the key. I slept in her bed. I could smell her. She had a painting she loved hanging on the wall opposite her bed. She told me that every night before she went to sleep, she looked at the painting. There was a door that was ajar and there was a piece of sky outside that door. The room itself was dark and you could see the traces of what was in the room. But you had to look hard to see what was there. She said she found things in that room. "Strange and awful things," she said. I wish to God she had paid attention to the blue sky that was outside that room.

I had a real boyfriend for a while. I started seeing him a few weeks after Carmen died. He was good to me and he made me laugh, and when he made love to me, he was tender and kind and affectionate. He said I cried in my sleep. He tried so hard to love me. For once, it wasn't just about catching the dragon. In the end, we broke up. He said I was too sad and that some day I wouldn't be sad anymore—and maybe then I would let someone love me. It was a kind thing to say—but it wasn't something that I believed would ever happen. Not to me.

I had loved only one person in my life. And that was my sister, the dragon I never caught. Some nights, I wake in the darkness, and I know I've been dreaming her. I see her sitting on the floor, her face illuminated by the light of the lamp in the room. She looks like an angel. I see her handing me the needle. I see me taking it. I hear her whispering in my ear. *Conrad, die with me.*

THE HURTING GAME

Because he died today, I'm drinking. I was never much of a recreational drinker, not before I met him. But right now I feel as if I have to do something, and the only thing that's entered my head is that I should have a drink. Just because it isn't an original thought doesn't make it a bad idea.

I get this phone call, Kathy's sweet voice telling me he's dead, no booze in the house, not a drop, drive to the liquor store, buy his favorite bourbon, pour it in a glass over ice, stare at it, hold it up, the ice cubes sparkling in the afternoon light. I drink. Then I drink another. That's what we did, we drank, me and him, when we were together.

I'm listening to Joni Mitchell and she's singing *Oh, I could drink a case of you*. Yeah, well, we both drank more than a case of each other. And what of it? I've been sitting here all afternoon, and it's night now. Tom's dead. And I'm supposed to be feeling something that resembles grief. But that's not what I'm feeling.

The first time he kissed me, he tasted like the bourbon he'd been drinking. Almost sweet. That's the first thing I thought when Kathy called me on the phone from his office. "He's gone," she said. *How? How?* But I didn't ask. I listened to her cry. "Shhh, shhh, baby." That's what he would have wanted me to tell her. I thought she'd sob forever. I hate to listen to people cry. All that hurt let loose, unrestrained, vulnerable, prideless, inarticulate, like howling dogs who have a sad sickness stuck inside them. Those howling dogs, they understand that if they are to survive, they have to howl in order to push that hurt out into the darkness of the sky. Howling may very well save dogs, but for people, crying isn't any good. I stopped crying a long time ago.

When my cell phone rang, it said: Tom Office. TOM1 was his private cell phone. I actually expected to hear his voice. I hadn't heard from him in over a month. That's the way it was with us. I wouldn't hear from him for a week or a month or two months and then I'd get a phone call from him. "Al," he'd say, "let's have a drink." My name is Michael—but he renamed me Al. "Mike-Al," he said one morning as we lay in bed. And then it just became Al. Half the time he called in the middle of the night. "Let's have a drink," he'd say.

And I'd say, "Now? It's one thirty in the morning."

"You were asleep?"

"What else would I be doing at one thirty in the morning?"

"I could think of a few things."

"I'm tired, Tom, it's late."

There would be silence on the phone—and I could tell he was a little hurt because when he called that late, I always refused to let him come over. I'd never been anybody's booty call, nobody's bitch.

"Okay," he'd say. "Tomorrow. At the Kentucky Club. Six o'clock?"

"Sure," I'd say. It was our private joke. He said he'd had a dream about me—and in that dream he walked into the Kentucky Club on Avenida Juárez and there I was at the bar, smiling, waiting for him. "That's where it began for us, babe. At the Kentucky Club."

"It was a dream," I said.

"You looked like an angel in that dream," he said. "A fucking angel."

I laughed. "So," I said, "the only way for me to arrive at angel status is to appear in your screwed-up dreams."

"Take it any way you can get it, babe."

I guess I got a kick out of the Kentucky Club thing. All it meant was that he'd pick me up at my place. Kentucky Club was code for home. Every time he arrived at my doorstep, he was all smiles and charm. He'd kiss me and say, "I missed you, babe." It annoyed me, all that affection pouring out of him. He made it all look so easy.

We'd laugh, we'd talk, we'd have dinner. He drank a lot. I drank with him. One time I wasn't in the mood to drink and I ordered a club soda. At the end of the evening, he said, "I feel lonely."

"Because I didn't drink with you?"

He nodded. He looked sad. I ordered a drink before we left. He kissed me in the car.

Mostly we'd wind up at my place. Sometimes we'd wind up in a nice hotel because he liked them and could afford them. But we never went to his place, not ever, and I didn't like that. I didn't even know where he lived. That put me at a disadvantage. You could tell a lot about a person when you knew where they lived, the neighborhood they chose, the yard they tended or didn't tend, the paintings they hung on their walls. Tom could study me through all the things I had in my house—and things I didn't have. He liked looking around my place. He said I had too many books.

"Look," I said, "I haven't read half of them."

It didn't make him feel any better. "That means you've read the other half."

"Guess so," I said.

"We got to get you a life," he said.

"Sometimes reading makes me feel alive."

"Like I said, we got to get you a life."

Tom and I, we had certain rules. I never asked about the details of his life. That was *his* rule. And we weren't ever, *not ever,* to bring up the word *love.* That was *my* rule. I wasn't going to get near that word. When he disappeared for a month or two, I never asked where he'd been. Sometimes he told me— sometimes he didn't. He had secrets. I let him keep them. I had my secrets too. So that's the way we played it.

I never figured out what we had, what I meant to him, what he meant to me. Not that I spent a lot of time thinking about it. I was busy counseling kids, some of them screwed-up as hell, wounded, some of them just wanting advice on where to go to college, some of them just wanting someone to talk to because they were already old and tired from being made invisible by the adults around them. And then there was night school at the university, trying to finish a degree in art. I loved art. It had everything to do with psychology. I was too fucking busy thinking about my last failed painting or my last conversation with a student or my last encounter with a lousy teacher who'd stopped caring or an out-to-lunch parent who had a hundred excuses as to why they didn't notice that their boy or their girl was doing drugs or having sex or engaging in behavior that was probably going to fuck them up even more. Yeah, I was too busy to analyze what Tom and I had. What we had, why did it have to have a name?

I met him five years ago. I was thirty. He was forty-five. He was handsome, just the other side of perfect. Once, he had been perfect. I sat across from him at a dinner party at a nice restaurant. One of my colleagues was married to an attorney, and they were celebrating ten years together. I didn't really understand marriage and ten years of it was either a miracle or hell pretending to be heaven. And there he was, one of the guests, Tom Espinosa, who didn't appear to have a hint of ethnicity left in his social make-up. A non-Mexican Mexican. He might as well have been a gringo. Hell, I was more Mexican than he was. It helped that my mother had been a Garcia. My father was a Steadman. Steadman genes and Garcia genes, all mixed-up to hell in my psyche. I got my mother's black eyes, my father's fair skin. My sense of irony I got from reading books and from some fucked-up relative a few generations back—probably on my father's side.

I was having a conversation with Susan in Spanish. Tom looked at me from across the table and said: "You one of those gringos who wants to be a Mexican?"

I looked at him and said, "I come by my Spanish honestly."

"What's that supposed to mean?"

"My mother was born in Mexico City."

He smiled. "My mother was born near the dump in Juárez."

"You win," I said.

He told me he was a criminal attorney. He was in the middle of a trial. It was a death penalty case and he believed in his client. I found that appealing. "Bad business, the death penalty. This is what passes for civilization." He dipped his finger in his drink. "You? What do you do?"

"I'm a high-school counselor," I said.

He smiled. "High-school counselor? Is that interesting?"

"My clients aren't criminals so maybe not so interesting."

He smiled again. All that smiling annoyed me. I was beginning to wonder if he didn't treat everyone as a potential juror. "Criminals aren't always that interesting." He was sipping on a glass of bourbon on the rocks. "You like kids?"

"Yeah. Something about them. I don't much care for their parents."

"You have any kids?"

"Nope."

"Planning on having any?"

I hated these questions. I got them all the time. "Nope, why would I want to become just like one of the parents I don't much care for?"

I don't remember what else we talked about. I noticed he drank a lot. But I also noticed he didn't seem to be getting drunk. Another thing I noticed: he was studying me. I didn't know what to think about that. He didn't seem like the kind of guy that would be interested in a guy like me.

At the end of the evening, he gave me his card. "Give me a call," he said. "We'll have a drink." He wrote down his cell number on his card. But just because he was easy on the eyes didn't mean I liked him enough to call him. There was something about him I didn't trust. He wore cologne. His hair was a little too combed. His clothes were a little too expensive. He wore a watch that he could pawn to buy a decent used car. He had too much money. I never cared much for people with money. They were a little too proud of themselves, too entitled. They never entertained the possibility that they might just be overpaid.

I never called him. He was the one who called me.

"How'd you get my cell?"

"You sound annoyed."

"Maybe."

"Susan gave it to me."

"Susan, yeah, well, she doesn't know how to keep other people's secrets."

"Your cell number's a secret?"

"Not anymore," I said. What I really wanted to say was that if I'd wanted him to have it, I'd have given it to him when we met.

"Wanna grab a drink?"

"Sure," I said. What the hell, there was nothing to lose. And then I regretted saying *sure* because I knew there was always something to lose.

We met at the bar at Café Central. It was six o'clock. He was talking on his cell, his coat hanging on his chair, his sleeves rolled up. His hair was more than a little uncombed and he looked tired but the whole look worked for him. He had a tattoo of a mermaid on his forearm. I sat down, almost smiled and let him finish his phone call.

He called the waiter over, raised his glass. I took the cue and ordered a glass of chard.

He clicked off his phone. "What are you, a girl? Drinking white wine?"

"If I was a girl," I said, "you wouldn't have asked me out for a drink."

He gave me a crooked smile.

"What makes you think I'm interested in men?"

"I'm not so sure you *are* interested in men. I just know you're interested in me."

"You sure about that?"

"You gave me your cell phone number, and when I didn't call, you came looking for me."

"And found you," he said.

"A real private eye." I stared at his tattoo. "I think better of you for that."

He stuck his arm out. "You want to touch it?"

"Okay, you just killed the moment."

"Are you always this hard?"

"I'm not exactly a walking Hallmark card."

"I thought gay men were supposed to be softer."

"Where do you go to get your information? Ever been to an S&M bar? Nothing soft about that."

"You frequent those places?"

"Nope. Ever hear of porn?"

"You don't strike me as a porn kind of guy."

"I'm not. I was curious when I was younger."

"And are you still curious?"

"I think I'm more curious about art."

He laughed. The drinks came. "Cheers," he said. "Try this." He pushed his drink toward me. I took a sip. "Nice," I said. I looked straight at him. "So, you're gay? Not gay? Curious? Bi? What?"

"Let's just say I like to sleep with people I find interesting."

"How many people do you find interesting?"

He didn't answer my question. He grabbed his drink. "Michael. You— *you're* interesting."

"And you arrived at this conclusion by doing research?"

"Don't need research. Sometimes I can just tell."

He tried to sleep with me that night.

I turned him down.

"What? You have a boyfriend?"

"No, but I think you're probably married."

"Divorced," he said.

Okay, so I let him kiss me. He was a good kisser, I'll give him that. Not that kissing was a particularly difficult art. Any fourteen-year-old boy could master that art in one evening if he had a willing partner. And I wasn't falling for Tom's crap. He was used to getting what he wanted and I wasn't about to whore myself out for a night just because the guy was a good kisser. Besides, I knew this guy was trouble. Sometimes you could sleep with a guy and that was that. But not this guy. This guy wanted more than a night. He wanted more than I was prepared to give. I knew that from the beginning. So I told him, "Listen, we need to have rules." I think he liked the idea of rules even more than I did.

One day, he called me in the middle of the afternoon. I had a crying student in my office. He'd shown me the belt marks on his calves and thighs, on his back. I wasn't exactly in a romantic frame of mine. "I'll call you back," I said. I stared into the hurt eyes of this boy, this boy who was more angel than I'd ever been or ever would be. For a second, I imagined myself grabbing the belt away from his father and giving him a dose of his own medicine. *How do you fucking like that, sir?*

This boy didn't need revenge. He needed something more, something I wasn't sure I could give him. But I wasn't the kind of guy that backed off. I was stubborn and I hated bullies. I looked at the boy straight in the face, his hurt pale blue eyes fighting to hold back the tears. "Danny, you can cry," I said.

"Do you?" he asked.

"Do I what?"

"Cry? Do you cry?"

"Yes," I said. "There's a lot of things to cry about." I lied. What was wrong with lying when you were trying to help someone?

So he nodded and his lips trembled and he hugged himself and he began to sob. I put my hand on his shoulder—touching was tricky business. "He'll never hit you again," I whispered. "I promise."

"My dad says he does it because he loves me."

"Your dad doesn't know a damn thing about love," I said.

I waited until Gina, the social worker, came by to pick Danny up. I didn't bother to call his father. I let social services take care of the matter. I gave Gina the report. I trusted her. She was as tough as she was beautiful—and, on the side, she was always willing to show me what I'd been missing. It was more of a joke than anything else.

Danny looked at me. "Where will I go? Where will they take me?"

"Wherever it is, you'll be safer. Gina won't let anything bad happen to you."

"What about my dad?"

Shit, why was it that kids like Danny were always trying to take care of a parent who didn't deserve to be taken care of, that didn't deserve their love, that didn't deserve to be called *Dad*? It was too common and too sad to talk about.

"I'll call your father," I said.

He nodded.

I didn't call him though. The truth was I was afraid of my own anger. I knew about fathers—the bad apples anyway. In my business I didn't get to hear about the good apples. Yeah, I knew about fathers. I'd had a father who loved me in exactly the same way Danny's father loved him.

I called Tom. "Still want to have a drink?"

I met him at the Dome Bar, downtown. I got there before he did. I ordered a glass of white wine and stared up at the Tiffany dome. It was so perfect and intricate and it filled the lobby of the hotel with light. I felt, for a moment, that I was in a church. But wasn't that what bars were—churches for people who'd lost their faith? Hell, I'm not sure I ever had any faith. I don't even think I believed when I was a boy. I remember making my first communion and thinking, *God can't possibly taste like this.* I looked up and Tom was standing there. "Hi," he said. He looked calm and happy and I wondered about that. He was always hiding something—but I didn't care about that. The part of him that was happy, that's the part I wondered about. I wasn't exactly sullen or morose or melancholy. But I wasn't exactly happy either.

"Hi back," I said.

"I wish I could kiss you right here," he said.

"We should have met at a different bar."

"Nah," he said. "I don't like the gay scene."

That made me laugh. "You like it well enough in bed."

"That's not the gay scene, that's two people touching."

"Two men touching," I said.

We sat and he drank and I watched him. He pointed at my glass of wine. "Still drinking those girl drinks?"

"Don't worry about it," I said.

He smiled.

I took him home. It was comforting to be held, to feel another man's hands on your body that made you feel, if even for an instant, that you mattered. It didn't have to be love. It just had to be something that made you feel alive. "You're quiet tonight," he said as we lay in the dark.

"I don't always have something to say."

"You're a mystery," he said.

"I don't mean to be."

"You can't help it. That's just the way you are. That's what I like about you. I could fall in love with a guy like you."

"That's a load of crap. You just think I'm pretty to look at."

"That's true, but that's not why."

"Let's not talk about it," I said. "You know the rules."

"Okay." He was quiet for a while and then said, "We make the rules and we can always change them."

He was wrong. The rules were ingrained in both of us. He just didn't know it. I took his hand and held it.

He spent the night. I made coffee in the morning and we took a shower together and I thought, *This is nice.* And, for a moment I thought that maybe—yeah, well, maybe.

I went to see Danny. He'd been temporarily placed in a foster home. He'd changed schools so his father couldn't find him. He was living in limbo, though perhaps that's where he'd always lived. Mr. and Mrs. Lucero, the foster parents, they were nice. Humble, good, decent, all of that. They doted over Danny as if he was their long lost grandson.

There was nothing fancy about the Lucero's home, but they weren't poor, not poor like so many people in this town were. The place was immaculately clean. Mrs. Lucero gave me coffee and she thanked me for saving this boy. That's how she put it. I assured her I wasn't in the business of saving anyone. She just smiled at me and condescendingly touched my cheek. I didn't mind. If someone was going to condescend to me, they might as well be sweet about it.

Danny seemed calm enough—except when he talked about his father.

"My mom died," he said. "My dad's been having a hard time."

"What about you, Danny?"

"I guess me too. He's sad. And he's mad. And he drinks."

"Bad combination of things," I said.

"My dad wants me back. He's hired a lawyer."

"Do you want to go back?"

He shook his head. "He says he won't hurt me anymore, but I know he will."

"You saw him?"

"Gina was in the room. She looked like she wanted to rip my father's throat out."

"Good for her."

"I don't know what to do, Mr. Steadman. My dad played like he was all nice but I could tell he was really mad. Gina could tell too."

"Smart girl." I shot him a smile. "Look, I have to make a phone call." I stepped out of the room and called Tom. "Can you talk?"

"Just got out of court. Walking towards my car."

"I need a lawyer."

"I'm your man."

"You don't practice family law, do you?"

"No. Hurts too goddamn much. Rather work with criminals."

"You know a good lawyer who does?"

"Sure."

"This boy," I said, "he can't pay."

Tom didn't hesitate. "No worries," he said.

"Thanks," I said. "I'll call you back."

I went back to the kitchen where Danny was sitting. Mrs. Lucero poured me another cup of coffee. It was terrible, her coffee, but I drank it with all the grace I could conjure. She stepped out of the room and left us alone so we could talk. "You have a number where you can be reached?"

"My dad turned off my cell."

"Let's go get you one."

We went to one of those places where you didn't need to buy a plan. I just filled the phone with plenty of minutes to get him through a month or so, and we were good to go. I punched his number into my cell phone and called him. "There," I said. "Now you have my number too. Call me if you need me."

"Mr. Steadman, you do this all the time?"

"No," I said.

"So why am I so fucking special?"

"Watch your mouth," I said.

We grabbed a bite to eat. He ate as if he'd never tasted a burger before. God, that boy had a hunger in him. It almost hurt to watch. "I'll be eighteen in three months. And I'm going away. And he'll never be able to find me."

"Where is that?" I asked.

"I don't know. I'm just going away."

I wanted to tell him that his father would always own a piece of him, that he would have dreams of his father chasing him, dreams of a father catching him and shoving him in a car and driving him back home, dreams where he could see every angry wrinkle on his father's face as he held up the belt like a whip. He would have those dreams. I knew all about them. I couldn't tell him that. He would find out on his own. He would have to learn how to save himself from everything he'd been through. Salvation existed in his own broken heart and he'd have to find a way to get at it. It all sucked, it sucked like hell. I didn't know what to tell him so I lied to him again. "He'll just be a bad memory one day."

He nodded. I don't think he really believed me, but he wasn't about to call me a liar.

Tom and I saw each other every night for a couple of weeks. We went to a few movies and held hands like high school boys. It all felt strange and foreign as if

I was inside one of the movies we were watching. We went for a long drive and listened to his favorite music and he wanted to talk. Talking could be so easy sometimes, and sometimes it could be hard, impossible. Sometimes the words were just there and sometimes they disappeared and there was no way to get at them. But, Tom, I don't think words ever disappeared for him.

He stopped the car and we took a walk in the desert. It was strange, the desert. I loved the stark landscape that refused to be tamed. I loved the mesquites, the cacti, the ocotillos that were like desperate fingers reaching out towards God, the rain bushes that held the smell of a summer storm in its stubborn sticky olive leaves. I thought of Danny. I thought of all the students who came to me. So many of them were like the plants that survived here, living without water. How did they do it? How did they survive? They came to me with a thirst in their eyes, a thirst, such a thirst, and I knew that I could never give them the rain they deserved, the rain they so desperately needed.

"Where are you, Al?"

"I was just thinking."

"Tell me."

"I was thinking about the desert."

"You love it, don't you? You love its austerity."

"Yes," I said. "I do."

"You could have been a monk."

"No, I couldn't."

"You're a better man than you think you are."

"What's that supposed to mean?"

"Who hurt you?"

"I don't want to talk about that, Tom."

"Okay," he said. We just walked through the arroyos. It was winter and we were both wearing coats and even though the breeze was cold, the sun was warm. "I love you," he said.

"You shouldn't," I said.

"Shouldn't love you or shouldn't say it?"

"Both."

"Why can't you just let yourself be loved?"

"Because," I said.

"Because? Because it hurts? So fucking what? Love's a hurting game, Al, don't you know that? But it's worth it. Sometimes it's worth it."

"No," I said. "I can't play that game."

"What do we have then?"

I took his hand. "We have touch. It's good. Let's just leave it at that."

We drove all the way to Marfa, Texas, and stayed at the Thunderbird, an overpriced place redone to look like a modern version of the 1950s motel. People were always trading in nostalgia. It was always good for business. It was such a cheap and easy thing to dress up the past and make it look beautiful.

Tom was so tender that night that I almost cried.

I always thought of men as being hard—maybe because *I* was hard. But there was a softness in Tom that betrayed his large masculine hands and his deep baritone voice. He knew something about love that I didn't. I don't know where he'd learned it, but it wasn't something you got from a book, not something you could learn in an online class, not something you could borrow. Maybe it was something you were born with. Some people knew how to love and some people didn't. Tom was the former. I was the latter. I didn't know which one of us had it worse.

I didn't hear from Tom for a long time after that. He dropped me off at my place and said, "I'll call you, babe." I knew he was going to disappear again. I wondered what it would be like to follow him to wherever it was he went. I had a funny feeling that it was a very dark place. Not that I minded dark places—it's just that I wasn't much of a follower.

I started working on a painting. It was for class but not really. I think it was just for me. I was trying to paint Tom and Danny. I had pictures of Tom on my cell phone and I e-mailed them to myself. I wasn't a great painter, and that was the truth. I wasn't terrible either. I had more imagination than skill. In the painting, Tom was driving a truck. And Danny was standing on the hood of the truck, his arms outstretched. The truck was floating in a blue, blue sky, and they were both happy. I think I liked the idea of the painting more than I liked the execution. But I wasn't finished and I was trying to make something that resembled real art. I knew I'd never be an artist. Look, I wasn't hurting anybody and working on a painting was good therapy. And I didn't have to sit across from a therapist and tell him the story of my life.

I got the urge one Friday night to go out to the bars. I lived in Sunset Heights, an old neighborhood that had old houses with a lot of class. It also had a lot of shabby houses that were falling apart. I liked the shabby houses. I liked that I could walk downtown. It was February and the night was cool, but it didn't feel like winter. It was as if spring was knocking at the door again. Not that I liked spring in El Paso. The winds came after us and left us beat up to hell, the taste of the desert sands being shoved down our throats by a God who didn't love us much.

When I got to one of the bars, I ordered a bourbon on the rocks and thought of Tom. I sat there and listened to the voices of the men around me and nodded my head to the beat of the music. I never felt like I belonged in these places. Maybe it was because I didn't want to belong. Gay guys weren't any different than straight guys. They all wanted you to be a part of a club, to be one of the boys. I don't remember ever wanting to be one of the boys. I didn't want to play for anybody's team, didn't want to go along with all the definitions of what men were supposed to be, definitions that were thrown around like baseballs in a ball park. Some guy sat next to me, smiled, told me his name. Sam. Latino, nice black eyes and hair as dark as the night. He offered to buy me a drink. He was good looking enough. I thought, what the hell. "Sure," I said.

We sat there and made small talk—and then he asked me, "You got a boyfriend?"

"Lots of them," I said.

He laughed. "I bet you do."

"So? You like to party?"

I knew exactly what that meant but I pretended not to know.

"Party?" I said.

"You know, party?"

"You mean like with a birthday cake?"

That pissed him off. He got the idea I was toying with him. "You always a wiseass?"

"Pretty much."

"Ever tried it?"

"Snow? Rock? Ecstasy? Nope."

"Not even a little 420?"

"Bad memories. It reminds me of the time in my life when I used to wake up and masturbate. Guess I've outgrown it."

He shrugged. "Live a little. Try it. We'll have fun."

"Don't want to try it."

"You don't know what you're missing."

"Look, I've never tried walking out in front of a bus. I'm pretty sure I know what would happen."

"Partying isn't like that."

"It's exactly like that."

"Not that you'd know."

"Yeah, not that I'd know."

He gave up on me pretty quickly. I wasn't what he was looking for. And he sure as hell wasn't what I was looking for. Not that I knew what that was.

I walked back home.

And there he was—Tom, his head bowed, sitting and shivering on my front steps.

"Tom?"

He didn't answer. He was shaking. "I'm tired," he whispered. He just sat there. He was all shadows in the light of my front porch.

I took him inside. He leaned on me, didn't say a word. He looked like he hadn't taken a shower in days. His face, scruffy and unshaven, his white shirt wrinkled and unbuttoned, his T-shirt soaked in sweat. He was trembling and hugging himself as he sat on a chair in my living room. I hadn't known until then that Tom was an addict. I didn't know what kind of addict, but he was definitely on something. "I need, I need more, I need—"

I took his hand and pulled him up from the chair. He didn't fight me. "Let's get you showered."

"And then will you get me some?"

I nodded. I got him into the shower. His clothes smelled rank. I put them in the washing machine. I got into the shower with him and washed him and he let me. He kept his head bowed. "You'll be okay," I said.

He started sobbing and couldn't stop.

"Shhh," I whispered.

"I'm sorry, babe." He kept whispering that. "So sorry, babe."

"There's nothing to be sorry for," I said.

I dried him off and led him to bed. "I need some more," he said.

I held him for a moment, tried to calm him. "I want some more." He kept repeating that. I sat up in bed.

"Are you leaving me?" he said.

"No. I'll be right back." I walked into the bathroom and looked through my medicine cabinet. I found what I was looking for. I took out my bottle of Xanax. I'd had problems sleeping, though I'd abandoned the Xanax almost as soon as I began to take it. Made me feel like shit when I woke up. I walked back to the bedroom. "Take this," I said.

He sat up naked in my bed. He had some bruises. He'd lost weight. It hurt me to look at him like that. "Put the pill under your tongue," I said. "It'll work faster that way." He didn't even ask what it was.

"Can I have a drink?"

"Sure," I said. Bourbon and Xanax wasn't a great idea. But it wasn't going to kill him. I brought him a drink. He sat there, staring out into the darkness, and slowly drank down his bourbon with hands that couldn't seem to stop trembling.

"Hold me," he whispered. I held him until he stopped shaking. It didn't take long before he fell asleep.

In the morning when I woke up, Tom was still asleep—dead asleep. I got up and took his clothes out of the washing machine and put them in the dryer. I put on some coffee and some music and read the news of the day online. I stared at the painting I was working on in my makeshift studio—a sunroom the previous owners had added onto the back of the house. It occurred to me that Tom would be hungry when he woke up so I went to the grocery store, bought a couple of steaks, some potatoes, some vegetables, a fucking cherry pie. I hated cherry pies. There was a reason for that. It had something to do with my father. But Tom—Tom loved cherry pies.

When I got back from the store, Tom was still asleep. He didn't wake until that evening. I was reading a book and he walked into my studio. He looked at the painting I was working on. "It's beautiful," he said.

I looked up and smiled at him.

"You don't know much about art, do you?"

He gave me a smirk and for a moment he looked like a boy, all innocent, not a trace of the life he lived on his face. "Al," he said, "your painting *is* beautiful. You're supposed to say thank you when someone gives you a compliment."

"I didn't get the memo."

He just shook his head and laughed. "I'm going to take a shower," he said. "You still have my toothbrush?"

"Yup. The red one. Your clothes are in the bedroom."

"Yeah, I know. Nice and folded."

"Don't get any ideas. I'm not your fucking wife."

He laughed.

We had dinner. We talked about stupid shit but didn't talk about what he'd been up to. Finally he looked at me and said, "Do you want to know?"

"Only if you want to tell me."

"I do things that are illegal."

"Yeah, I get that."

"No, Al, it's not just that I do drugs."

"You don't do heroin, do you?"

"No."

"Good. I hate heroin."

He just looked at me.

"I lost someone," I said.

"Who?"

"Do I have to tell?"

"Tell me, Al."

"My mom." After twenty years it still hurt. I felt the tears right there, right *there*, and I hated them, hated that they hadn't forgotten me and still lived in me, hated Tom for reminding me of all those awful days, those days when love left me and all that remained was an addict mother and the cruelest father in the whole fucking universe.

Tom put his hand on my cheek. "I'm sorry, babe."

"Yeah, well, life is a little bigger than all of us."

He nodded. "I'm in over my head, Al."

"I'll help you stop."

"No, you don't understand. It's not just about my little addict self. I got in with some people. I don't think I can get out. I can't tell you. If they knew, Al, if they knew I had someone like you in my life. If they knew. They'd hurt you, Al. Why do you think I got a divorce? That's what I'm talking about."

"Tom. What the fuck are you saying?"

In the morning, when I woke up, Tom was gone. He left a note:

> Babe, for the past five years, we've been good, haven't
> we? There wasn't anybody else but you. Just you. First
> time I saw you sitting across from me at that dinner,
> you were talking to Susan, and there was something

about you that was so beautiful and alive and perfect. The problem, of course, is that you don't know that. Maybe that's part of what makes you so beautiful. I'm sorry I'm so fucked up. But we're all fucked up, don't you know that? Maybe that's the key to it all, that we're all fucked up and the only way we survive is to do the love thing, you know? You told me once that you didn't do the love thing. Yeah, I think I called it the hurting game. Yeah, love hurts, Al. And you don't want to have anything to do with hurt. You don't have a choice, babe. You don't. Al, it's not love that's the hurting game. It's life. Life is the hurting game. Don't you know that, babe? Oh, babe, don't you know that?

I didn't know if I would ever see Tom again.

Sunday evening, I got a call from Danny. "I'm going away," he said.

"Danny, you can't survive out there."

"My dad, he found me. I don't know how he found out, but he found me when I was leaving my new school. He took me back home. He beat the holy crap out of me. Lucky for me that the sonofabitch got good and drunk and passed out."

"I'll call the police."

"No. Screw that. I'm getting the hell out of this town."

"They'll find you."

"No one can stop me."

"Where are you?"

"I'm at the bus station."

"You don't have any money, do you?"

He didn't say anything.

"I'll be right there," I said. When I got to the bus station, I spotted

Danny. His face was swollen and both of his eyes were black and blue. He kept holding his ribs and I knew that there were bruises everywhere beneath his clothes. I brought him home. He didn't even have a backpack on him. "Can you trust me?" He nodded. "Good."

"I'm hungry," he said. I sent out for a pizza and he ate it all. Every fucking bit of it. When he finished, I said, "Let's go to a hospital."

"What?"

"Trust me."

I took him to the emergency room. I wasn't his guardian. The lady behind the glass window said, "Need parental permission. Can't take him."

"Look," I said, "do you see him? I'm his high-school counselor. His father did that to him."

I called Gina. She gave the woman a piece of her mind. So fierce and beautiful, that woman. They took care of Danny. He had a broken rib. The police were called. I was with Danny as he lay in a bed. God, his body, his poor boy body, God, I didn't know how he'd managed to walk to a bus station, didn't know how he'd managed to stay sane and good, but I *did* know that this boy wanted to live.

"Take pictures," I told the police. "Take fucking pictures."

The attorney Tom had referred me to was good as gold. As it turned out, Danny had an aunt, his mother's sister. She lived in Boulder, Colorado. She was more than happy to take him in. "I've tried to call him so many times, but his father would never let me see him." She wept on the phone, but the tears weren't sad ones, and I knew she was a good woman and that Danny would be safe with her and that was all that mattered. Maybe Tom was wrong. Maybe not everyone in the world was fucked up.

A week after Danny had called me, I took him to the airport. His aunt Margaret paid for the ticket. He looked at me with his sad pale eyes as we said goodbye. He leaned into my shoulder and sobbed quietly. "I love you, Mr. Steadman." I wanted to tell him that he didn't know a goddamned thing about me, that I was just this man who was ordinary in every way, who struggled with things that were not important, a guy who had a hard time getting close to people. I wanted to tell him that I wasn't worth admiring. So I just took him by the shoulders and looked him straight in the eye. "Danny, people shouldn't get extra credit for doing what they're supposed to do. No one should get extra credit for doing their job."

He smiled. God, I hadn't seen that boy smile like that, not ever. "Mr. Steadman, I'm on to you." He hugged me, then walked toward the escalators.

He turned around and waved.

I waved back, then slowly made my way to the parking lot.

I don't normally read the paper. I'm a get-the-job-done kind of guy, no wasting time. But that day, I got up and discovered I was out of coffee. So I stopped off at Starbucks on my way to work. Never did the drive-in thing. I liked walking in and ordering my coffee from a human being instead of a voice that came out of a speaker. As I stood in line, there he was—Tom!—on the cover of the *El Paso Times*. ATTORNEY FAKES HIS OWN DEATH. I took the newspaper and all of a sudden, I started laughing. I couldn't stop fucking laughing. I don't remember ever having laughed like that. I had to sit down, and when I finally calmed down, I had to wipe away my tears. *Tom, Tom, Tom, what have you done?*

I read a little piece of the story. He'd been hiding out in Juárez and had bribed some cop to place his passport in the pocket of a dead body. I laughed at his quote: "I got tired of being dead, so I just decided to raise myself back to life."

They arrested him at the border.

He was sitting in the county jail.

All this time, I'd imagined his last moments, a gun pointed at him from some assassin hired by the drug lords he'd gotten in with. I'd even had dreams about it, had dreamed his frightened eyes.

There was no answer when I called his office. I called his legal secretary's number on my phone. I heard her voice. "Kathy?"

"Yes."

"It's Michael."

"Michael! Oh, Michael! Did you read the paper?"

"Yes. I haven't read all the fine print."

"God, Michael."

"He's alive, Kathy, that's all that matters."

She started to cry.

"Shhh, it's okay, honey. It's gonna be okay."

"He's going to have to do some time, Michael."

"Doesn't matter. Listen, can you get me in to see him?"

"Sure," she whispered. "I think I can manage that."

"Good," I said.

I hung up the phone. I called in sick. I took a walk in the desert. At around three in the afternoon, I walked into the Camino Real Hotel and went into the Dome Bar. I stared at the Tiffany dome. I ordered a bourbon on the rocks. A double. I smiled as I took a sip. God, I was so happy. I lifted my glass up to the light. Just then my cell phone rang. It was Kathy. "You can see him this afternoon. You have to be at the county jail at four. I'll meet you there."

"Thanks," I said.

"He loves you. You know that, don't you?"

"Yeah," I whispered. "I've always known that."

I looked at my watch. It was three-fifteen.

I sipped on my drink and thought of how Tom had laughed at me the first time we had a drink together, *What are you, a girl? Drinking white wine?* So I'm sitting here, drinking bourbon, thinking of him, my Tom. I'm thinking, *God, he's not dead.* And I'm smiling. God, I'm smiling like I've never smiled before. I can almost hear his voice as he tells me about his dream, *You were sitting at the bar of the Kentucky Club and you looked like a fucking angel.* I'm imagining me sitting there and I do, I do feel like a fucking angel, and I'm waiting for him, and then I picture him walking in, and he says to me, "See, babe, it's true, everything begins and ends at the Kentucky Club."

I look at him and say, "No, not everything, just your dreams."

OTHER BOOKS BY BENJAMIN ALIRE SÁENZ

NOVELS

Carry Me Like Water (Hyperion)

The House of Forgetting (HarperCollins)

In Perfect Light (HarperCollins)

En el tiempo de la Luz (Rayo/HarperCollins)

Names on a Map (Harper Perennial)

SHORT STORIES COLLECTIONS

Flowers for the Broken (Broken Moon Press)

POETRY

Calendar of Dust (Broken Moon Press)

Dark and Perfect Angels (Cinco Puntos Press)

Elegies in Blue (Cinco Puntos Press)

Dreaming the End of War (Copper Canyon Press)

The Book of What Remains (Copper Canyon Press)

YOUNG ADULT

Sammy & Juliana in Hollywood (Cinco Puntos Press)

He Forgot to Say Goodbye (Simon & Schuster)

Last Night I Sang to the Monster (Cinco Puntos Press)

Aristotle & Dante Discover the Secrets of the Universe
(Simon & Schuster)

CHILDREN'S BOOKS

A Gift from Papa Diego (Cinco Puntos Press)

Grandma Fina and Her Wonderful Umbrellas (Cinco Puntos Press)

A Perfect Season for Dreaming (Cinco Puntos Press)

The Dog Who Loved Tortillas (Cinco Puntos Press)

CPSIA information can be obtained
at www.ICGtesting.com
Printed in the USA
LVHW030958270219
608907LV00003B/4